SU

Life seemed very good to Staff Nurse
Charis Littleton: a happy family background, a job she loved in a lovely
university town, and her fiancé Neil
Chambers. But wasn't it all a little *too*
pleasant and uneventful? It was strange
how her feelings had altered since she
met surgeon Guy Morland...

Janet Ferguson was born at Newmarket, Suffolk. She nursed as a V.A.D. during the Second World War, then became a medical secretary working in hospitals in London and the provinces and (more latterly) in Brighton, Sussex, where she now lives. She has had eighteen novels published—seven of them being Doctor Nurse Romances. These, she says, she finds the most satisfying and interesting to plot: 'I couldn't be happy unless I had a story to weave. My characters are nearly as real to me as my friends and colleagues, several of whom are nurses and who—sometimes unwittingly—supply me with the kind of material I can use!' Janet Ferguson's recent titles include *Sister on Penhallow Ward* and *Nurse on Livingstone Ward*.

SURGEON ON CALL

BY
JANET FERGUSON

MILLS & BOON LIMITED
15-16 BROOK'S MEWS
LONDON W1A 1DR

An abbreviated version of this story first appeared in Woman's Weekly as a serial in 1986.
First published inHardback in Great Britain 1987 by Mills & Boon Limited

This edition 1987

C Janet Fergerson 1986

Australian copyright 1987
Philippine copyright 1987

ISBN 0 263 75742 0

Set in Monotype Times 10.4 on 10.4pt
03-0587-59108

Typeset in Great Britain by
Associated Publishing Services
Printed and bound in Great Britain by
Collins, Glasgow

CHAPTER ONE

THE Hospital stood in the heart of the university town. It faced on to Princes Parade, the most beautiful street in Seftonbridge; its tower block vied with the dreaming spires.

Three floors up on Athelstone Ward, which was Male Orthopaedic, Charis Littleton, senior staff nurse, was hurrying into the cloakroom, reaching for her navy overcoat. In the ordinary way she had lunch upstairs in the nurses' dining-room, but today she wanted to do some shopping; it was only three weeks to Christmas; she had one or two quick purchases to make.

In a matter of minutes she was down in Reception, crossing the yard to the gate, cutting along St Margaret's Street in a bitter north-east wind, to Carter & Mayhews, the big department store chain. She went straight to the jewellery department, where she hoped to be able to buy some earrings for her married sister; she knew the sort Nan wanted—the chunky, dangling kind for evening wear.

It was while she was turning the display stand round that she noticed the dark-haired man in a sheepskin jacket standing at a counter in the more expensive section. He was a very noticeable kind of man, tall and lean-faced, and he had an air of elegance that somehow drew the eye. He was examining several necklaces, they looked to be of blue stones. He was probably buying a present for his girl-friend, or his wife; Charis judged him to be around thirty-four or five. The assistant, with coned greyish hair, was clearly under his spell. She was smiling coquettishly, dangling the necklaces, draping them at her throat. Then two things happened, one after the other. The assistant was called to the phone . . . from where Charis stood, she could just glimpse her with her back to the counter, nodding her head and stroking the round of her hip. It was when Charis glanced back at the man that the second thing happened . . . she was just in time to see him pick up one of the necklaces and thrust it into the pocket of his coat. She heard her own gasp . . . she couldn't believe . . . was it true? Had she really seen it? She knew she had, she wasn't mistaken. He moved, he was coming her way. She was right in line with the doors to the street, she was stung into action . . . foolish action. She stepped straight into his path. The force with which they collided knocked out her breath in a grunt. He swore, she heard him, she felt him holding her, gripping her upper arms.

'For Pete's sake, can't you look where . . . '

She choked and found her breath. 'I saw you, I saw you take it . . . that necklace, I saw you take it!' Her words were scarcely above a whisper, but several shoppers turned round.

'*What* did you say?' One of his hands manacled her wrist. Looking up into his long, dark, totally baffled face, she had a terrible feeling of hideous, creeping doubt. Could she have made a mistake? Was she wrong? Had she hallucinated? Was she wrong . . . was she . . . *was* she? Had he really put out his hand and slipped that string of bright blue stones into his jacket pocket? She knew he had, she wasn't mistaken; he was putting on an act.

'You took that necklace!' And now her voice accused.

More people were turning to stare, several gathered round. Charis saw none of them, all she saw was the man in front of her—face tight, mouth compressed, grey eyes contemptuous. 'Come with me!' Still holding her wrist, he marched her over the carpet to the counter where two necklaces lay by their velvet-lined boxes, to the counter where the assistant was still on the phone. She was finishing, she replaced the receiver, she turned and smiled at the man.

'Oh, I thought I saw you leaving, sir. Perhaps, after all, you feel this,' she pointed to one of the necklaces, 'might be a fairly good match. I personally feel . . . ' She stopped as she saw his hand make a staying gesture.

'Will you explain to this young woman,' he injected forcibly, 'why I was perfectly entitled to take this away with me?' His hand plunged into his pocket and came out with the necklace. He swung it to and fro under Charis's nose.

'Why, because . . . because it belongs to you, sir!' The assistant looked pink and shocked. She stared at Charis. 'The gentlemen wanted to buy one exactly like it. Unfortunately we didn't . . . don't have one, at least not at the moment. I intended to wrap his up for him, but then I was called to the phone. You don't mean to say . . . you couldn't have thought . . . ' even her neck went pink, 'you couldn't have thought he *stole* it!' She turned horrified eyes to him, then back to Charis, who stood there feeling sick. She struggled for words, but they wouldn't come. The man's face seemed miles away . . . it seemed high up, close to the ceiling, creased and angry and dark.

'I made a mistake, I'm terribly sorry, I jumped to the wrong conclusion! I ought to have realised, ought to have known . . . ' she sounded like an old woman. 'I hope you'll feel able to accept my apology.'

And now his face was all too clear, there was no longer any doubt that this awful scene was really happening; his words fell about her like rocks. 'Your sense of duty, of law and order, does you credit,' he snapped, 'but be a little more circumspect the next time you feel inclined to try your hand at a citizen's arrest!'

'I'm so . . . ' she began, but he swept her aside, and the necklace back into his pocket.

'Excuse me, I'm late.' He thanked the assistant, and once more proceeded at a swift pace towards the exit doors.

There was a chair against the counter, and Charis sank down on it, not sure that her legs would support her; her knees had turned to foam. One or two people spoke to her, some blamed her, some did not. The assistant was putting the necklaces back into their boxes, pressing the lids down, making clicking snaps. 'You made a shocking mistake, you know,' she said censoriously. Another woman, one of the group who had witnessed the little scene, was even more scathing. 'I can't think why you stuck your neck out,' she breathed. 'Places like these have their own ways of spotting would-be thieves.' She turned up her collar and went away blowing her nose.

Charis had to move, she had got to move, she couldn't sit here like this, pilloried, with everyone 'pelting bricks'. Somehow or other she made her legs work, and they got her out into the street. The wind hit her sideways on, she welcomed its freezing blast. Anything was better than that stifling store. How could I have done such a thing? she thought. How could I have done it, for even if he had been, really had been a thief, how could I have been such an idiot as to try to stop him myself? I acted on impulse, a kind of outrage. I didn't stop to think. I just rushed in like a silly fool, and he hadn't done a thing . . . not a thing wrong. She began to feel ill again.

I shall never tell anyone about it, she thought . . . no one, except Neil, of course. That man . . . his face. He was furious! If looks could fire a gun I'd be in the hospital morgue by now, stretched out on a slab. All I hope is, all I pray is, I'll never see him again, and the odds are against my doing so, because Seftonbridge is huge. And as for the store, I don't have to go inside it again for ages, I can easily get Nan's earrings somewhere else.

As she turned down St Margaret's Street she felt the wind behind her, pushing and shoving, speeding her on . . . on towards the hospital, on and on, and farther away from Carter & Mayhew's store . . . on and on, and closer, had she known it, with every step she took, to a tall dark man in a sheepskin coat.

When she saw him, for she could hardly fail to, he was at the hospital gates, talking to Soames, the porter, in his lodge. His back was towards her, and she stopped, praying he wouldn't turn round. He didn't, he was following Arthur Soames' pointing arm and directions, then he strode across the yard to Admin Block.

Charis watched him go. 'Mr Soames, who was that?' she asked, and her face had paled. Soames grimaced, he was trying to get the top off his thermos flask; his lodge was draughty, and his feet were blocks of ice.

'He's not one of us, dear—at least, not yet,' the flask was unscrewed at last, 'he's one of the candidates for the Orthopaedic Registrar's job, you know. He's the last on the list, there were five this morning. Sir Rodney's on the panel. You can't have forgotten the interviews, you being on the Ortho floor.'

'No, I hadn't forgotten them. Thank you, Mr Soames.' Somehow she managed to smile, and cross the yard, and get up to the ward. She took off her hat and coat, tidied her hair, and pinned on her cap. It wasn't until she reached Sister's office that realisation struck, like a swinging axe, and she went hot and cold in waves.

He would get the job, she knew he would. In no way was she clairvoyant, but there were times, nevertheless, when she could hazard an accurate guess as to how a situation would turn out. He would get it, he was a winner type, he would walk away with the job. She could see him in her mind's eye, shaking hands with the panel, looking dark and forceful, and agreeing his starting date.

'Can you sign this requisition, Staff?' Jean Pelham, the third-year nurse, put her head round the door, and went in when she saw Charis nod. It was a requisition for light bulbs and a new lamp for the ward desk. Life had to go on, work had to proceed. Charis did her signing; retaining one form, she sent the rest to Stores.

The afternoon was a busy one, as Sister was off duty. This meant that as senior staff nurse, Charis was in charge. There were people to see—the hospital chaplain, the librarian bringing new books; there was visiting-time, and two sets of relatives wanting a word with her; a patient for hip replacement was settled in. Throughout all this there was no clear time to dwell on the scene in the shop, nor on what was going on downstairs in Admin Block. It was there in her mind, though, all the time, sitting there waiting to spring. Trying to keep it at bay was like pushing against a door that refused to shut; it was tiring to say the least.

At four-thirty she went into the office to work out duty rosters. She had scarcely begun before Robert Peele, Sir Rodney Barks' houseman, projected himself excitedly into the room. 'If it's tea you're after, Rob,' said Charis, 'you'll have to use the machine. The ward teas went out an hour ago.'

'I'm not on the scrounge, I'm the bearer of news.' Charis's heart gave a jump. 'I've just been introduced to our new Registrar who'll be joining us at the end of January.'

'I see,' she said, and smiled at Rob, amazed at how calm she felt—or perhaps 'resigned' was the better word, after all she had known it would happen. She could even stop thinking about herself and spare a thought for Rob. Accord between Registrars and housemen was very necessary, if the patients' best interests were to be served. 'Tell me more,' she said brightly—over-brightly. Rob sat on the end of the desk.

'He looks hard to me,' he chewed his lip, 'a nail and chisel type. He's not bad-looking, tall and dark, handshake like a vice. He'll be good at his job, and that's for sure, he's got that kind of aura. His name's Morland, Guy Morland, and why I've chased up here is to warn you that Barks is showing him round, I heard them talking about it. This might be them now,' he cocked an ear, and they both heard the distant thud of the lift's arrival, the drooling back of its doors. 'They're bound to go into Docherty first. I'm off, I don't want to be caught.' Rob scudded off at great speed, en route for the Duty Room, with its access to the second flight of stairs.

Charis stared at the door. She wished he had stayed. Then she gave herself a shake. It was childish to panic, to feel that she couldn't face Guy Morland. She had got to, it was part of her job, there were no two ways about it, and anyway there was always a chance that he might not recognise her. Her outdoor coat had been concealing, and the navy pillbox hat had surely covered most of her hair; she looked different in dress and cap, and her face was hardly the traffic-stopping kind. She got to her feet, smoothing her dress of crisp lilac cotton; her dark gold hair in its thick French pleat lay tidy under her cap; her belt buckle was dead centre; she could see herself reflected in the glass-fronted cupboard set on the opposite wall. I'll pass, she thought, on the job I look older. I'm not who you think I am, Mr Guy Morland. She sat down and waited for him.

When the two surgeons came in she was ready for them, but none of her careful preparedness was any use when, once again, she came face to face with the man who had just been appointed Senior Registrar.

There he was, crossing the room—jet-haired and straight-featured, tall and broad-shouldered in his exquisite suit, moving easily, wearing his maleness like a badge. There was no means of telling if he recognised her, or at least, there wasn't at first, but as Sir Rodney introduced them, as her hand met his, as his quizzing eyes under lifted brows met hers fairly and squarely, she knew he knew *exactly* who she was.

He said nothing apart from the trite words that follow on introductions. His voice—deep, rich, melodious, complemented the harshness of his set expression, the hard line of his jaw. But that same voice could roughen in anger . . . remembering when it had done so, Charis quickly transferred her gaze to Sir Rodney Barks.

'Got time to come into the ward with us, Staff?' Sir Rodney boomed in her ear. He was a short, square, mastiff man, renowned for his surgical skills, and for his moods, which were unpredictable.

'Yes, of course, sir.' He was standing close, he was roughly Charis's height, which was five foot three, and the scent of his buttonhole—a clove carnation today—filled her nostrils, she breathed it in deeply. Deep breathing cured many ills, helped one over bad patches, calmed the nerves. She led the way into the ward.

It looked untidy, higgledy-piggledy, but then it always did. How could it be otherwise with so much in it, so many splints and frames, and hoists and pulleys, wires and weights, and varying types of beds—not to mention the wheelchairs and crutches, and patients in weight-bearing plasters who were levering out to the bathrooms, and loos, and back.

'It's twenty-eight bedded, not including the side-wards,' Sir Rodney explained. 'The Female Ward, Docherty, is a replica of this one, roughly half is given over to elective surgery, the rest to accident cases. There was talk at one time of upgrading us, dividing the wards into bays, but the idea was shelved, and I can't say I mind. I like two rows of beds and a straight run through them, and I'm sure the nursing staff do.' he glanced at Charis, but without waiting for any reply or reaction, he rapped on the ward desk and asked for some notes. Learner Nurse Adams, who was filing X-rays, nearly jumped out of her skin, but she found the case-notes and handed them over to him. The desk—more properly called the Nurses' Station—provided a suitable base from which all patients could be readily observed. It was commodious too, like a mini-office, facilitating the storage of charts and notes in portable trucks and racks. 'You might like to come and meet these two patients,' Sir Rodney brandished the notes, 'they'll still be here when you come in January, so you might as well make their acquaintance.'

'Good idea, I'd like to,' Guy Morland said equably, and they all three made their way to the bedside of Mr Ivyson, whom Guy Morland had noticed as soon as they entered the ward. William Ivyson had undergone a spinal operation, involving the fusing together of two adjacent vertebrae, after long-standing illness had interfered with the function of the cord. He lay in a plaster shell, called a bed, which was moulded to his back. The 'bed' was mounted on a wooden stand, while his head and heels and arms were supported by pillows; he was seven days post-op. He had fallen into a light doze, and Charis felt rather vexed at the thought of him being roused for little more than a social call. Her vexation showed, but perhaps she had really made no attempt to hide it. Sir Rodney's hand, like a well-groomed paw, drew her away from the bed.

'All right, m'dear . . . caught your drift. We'll leave him to rest, if you like. Sufficient to say,' he turned to Guy Morland, 'that he's adapted well to his bed, *and* to all the restrictions it entails. He's doing

well, so far. His flesh wound should heal in a week or
ten days, but good bony fusion could take fourteen or
sixteen weeks.'

'A long business,' Guy Morland observed, as they
moved back to the desk. Charis noticed him give a
backwards glance at the in-shell Mr Ivyson, who
looked, as he himself had ruefully told Sister yesterday,
like a beached turtle, lying helpless on his back.

'Come May Day he won't know himself,' Sir Rodney
insisted, 'he'll be joining the morris dancers on Trinity
Green.'

Guy Morland's comment was stopped at source by
the croaking of Sir Rodney's bleep. He reached for
the telephone on the desk, dragging it to his ear.
'Barks here . . . who wants me?' Charis and Guy
Morland waited, but not for long; the elder man's,
'Yes, yes, I'm coming now,' reached them before he
swung round, fleshy face moving in folds. 'Gotta go,
crushed thorax in A and E. Join me down there,
Morland. No, not now, see the knee patient first. Staff
will fill you in.' Off he went, taking short steps, and
limping imperceptibly; as a young man he had suffered
from polio.

To be left with Guy Morland was daunting; it was
also a kind of challenge. He had about him an air
of . . . 'Well, let's see what you're made of', and he
stood there waiting, half-turned from her, boldly
surveying the ward. For a new man, and not even
that yet, since he hadn't officially started, he was
plainly not short on confidence. Charis held out Paul
Dobson's notes, he unfolded his arms and took them.

'He's a footballer, sir,' she started to say, but he
put up a staying hand.

'There's no need to "sir" me,' he said aloofly. 'Mr
Morland will do.' He was studying the notes, eyes cast
down, straight nose looking long, and somehow or
other his words which should have made her feel more
at ease tended to have the opposite effect.

He was condescending, she decided, hating the fact that she flushed so easily and showed her discomfiture. 'Paul's a footballer,' she began again, 'he plays for Seftonbridge County, or perhaps I should say that he *did* play, until his motorbike accident. He smashed up his right knee, had a transverse fracture with separation. Reduction wasn't feasible, so the patella was removed.'

'Oh dear, so amen to his footballing days.' Guy Morland's eyes met hers for a fleeting moment over the top of the notes.

'It looks that way, yes.' For some reason or other, she couldn't say 'Mr Morland'. They began to walk down the length of the ward.

'A knee without a patella is often good, but seldom pergect.' He kept his voice low as they neared Paul Dobson's bed.

Tousled, freckled and not very happy, Paul was sitting up, right leg encased in a long plaster cylinder. He was eating an orange which matched his hair, and reading the midday edition of the *Seftonbridge Times*, which his twin brother had brought in at visiting time. To see a VIP at this time of day was the last thing he had expected—that much was plain by the hasty way he scooped up the pungent orange-peel and dropped it down on the floor by his can of Coke.

Before Charis could so much as open her mouth, Guy Morland explained who he was, and why he was there; he put the boy at ease. She noticed, and this was often the case with medical people, that he showed an entirely different side when talking to a patient. He levelled with Paul, he pulled his leg—metaphorically, of course—he mentioned football, which could have been a disaster but somehow was not. It was that old thing called a bedside manner, and perhaps it meant very little, but who cared about that if it cheered the patient up.

Just before they left him, Paul even managed to

joke. When Guy Morland said: 'See you in January,' Paul replied: ''Fraid so, sir. By then they'll have got me knitting, I expect!' And he nodded to bed number twelve, where old Mr Simmons, bearded and earnest, and grunting in numbers, was at work on a scarf as long as his splinted leg.

Guy Morland laughed. 'There are worse fates, surely?'

'Yes, like getting spliced!' Paul's left eye and half his face screwed up in a wink.

'Who was he getting at, do you know?' Guy Morland asked as they neared the doors. He was looking at Charis—down at her; he was over six feet, she thought. Neil was tall, but his height didn't overwhelm her as this man's did. She wondered why this was, then applied herself to answering his question.

'He was having a knock at me, Mr Morland.' The name tripped from her lips easily enough at this juncture, and she liked the sound of it. She decided that it suited him. 'I'm getting married next year.' And she liked the sound of that even more; she was happily engaged, firmly committed, and it meant a great deal to her. Neil was a chartered surveyor, he worked in her father's office. They had met eighteen months ago, and had got to know one another gradually, which was surely the best way of all. She was in no great hurry to be married, but she wanted to know it was coming. She wanted a home and family of her own.

Guy Morland said something she couldn't catch; it was noisy in the corridor. All the ancillary rooms gave off sounds; there were swishings from the sluice, the chink of teaspoons from the kitchen, the clang of metal bowls from the treatment room, the banging down of lids. Nurses passed and re-passed, glimpses of white-capped heads, the flit of a mauve uniform dress, the sight of a dark-clad leg and low-heeled shoe, were all part of the five o'clock scene.

As they passed through the swing doors into the comparative quietness of the landing, Charis felt impelled to say something about the incident in the store. She felt she couldn't ignore it—it seemed the right thing to do to bring it up and clear the air, and make her peace with him. No right-minded person liked working under a cloud. 'Mr Morland,' she began, 'I would just like to say how very sorry I am about what hap . . . ' and then she stopped, for his hand was up again, palm towards her in the way of a policeman's halt. She stared at it, then up at him. His face was expressionless.

'You've apologised once,' he said curtly, 'there's no need to do so again.' And with that the matter was closed, slammed shut, tightly, hermetically sealed. And Charis was rocked back on her heels.

She said: 'I see,' then heard herself, in a shaken flustered voice, explaining the layout of the various rooms that comprised the Ortho floor. She was determined not to let him see how his snub had affected her. She talked on and on at random, she dared not look at him. 'We have two theatres,' she finished, 'but they're in the main theatre block, one floor down. Actually, we find . . . ' Once again he cut her off short.

'Sir Rodney told me all that on the way up here, Staff.' He walked to the head of the stairs, no doubt expecting her to follow. She did, involuntarily at first, and then she stood her ground.

'Then he probably also told you,' she said, raising her voice a little, 'that our Accident Unit is on the ground floor, across the yard in the tower block. I ought to get back to the ward, Mr Morland. Can you find your own way, do you think?'

There were seconds of silence, then he swivelled round, one hand on the rail. Her tone had been civil, but he got the message. He looked at her carefully, a small pulse flicking away at the angle of his jaw, eyes narrowed, lips just starting to move. 'I should think I might manage that,' he said. 'I'm fairly used to hospitals.' And then he was jolting down the stairs, shoulders and seal-dark head vanishing from sight as he reached the bend.

I hope he jolly well loses his way, or slips up in the yard, Charis thought unhappily, as she hurried back to the ward. He was 'fairly used to hospitals' . . . he was fairly sarcastic too, standing there in his fabulous suit, looking like Royalty. Yet fairness made her admit that perhaps one couldn't really blame him for wanting to get his own back by making her feel a clot. She had called him a thief in a crowded store, less than five hours ago. He wouldn't forget that easily, but she tried her level best to forget *him,* when she saw how late she was.

She was supposed to be off duty, what was she thinking about? She should have handed over to the junior staff nurse half an hour ago. She was calling for Neil at Hansons, they were driving out into the Fens to have supper with her half-sister Nan and Harold, Nan's nurseryman husband. Nancy and Harold Roffey had brought Charis up.

Neil was a great one for being on time—a facet of his character which Charis respected, and so did her father, who was going to make him a partner, when the new office at Kingsford got under way. Hanson & Sons, Chartered Surveyors, Land Agents and Valuers, was one of the most up-market firms in the whole of East Anglia. There were three partners, and Cedric Littleton, Charis's widower father, was the senior partner, the captain of the ship. He was sixty-nine, but had no plans for retiring in the near future. The firm was his life, his advice to clients on land and property values was spot on target, and very zealously sought.

He was easing his black Rover away from the office forecourt when he saw Charis waving from the other

side of the road. He managed to stop and wait until
she had threaded her way through a stream of bicy-
cling undergraduates, and leapt past a newspaper van.
As she reached the car he rolled the window down.
'Had a good day?' he asked her. The street lamp
shadowed her face, made a spun gold aureole of her
hair. She was still in uniform, and her navy coat,
belted tightly in, made her look more like a schoolgirl
then the twenty-four years she was. A heavy bag
dragged at her shoulder, and he viewed it with distaste.
What had she done, he wondered, with the genuine
leather bag he had given her in the summer . . .
why use that thing like a sack?

'A mixed day,' said Charis, not minding his disap-
proval. She was beginning to know her father and
love him as he was, and goodness knows it had taken
long enough.

'Neil's just signing his letters,' he told her. He began
to pull on his gloves. 'And there's someone waiting to
see him, he's likely to be late.'

'I've got a book, I can sit and read.' She smiled,
and his frown disappeared. When Charis smiled her
plainish features lit up into beauty. 'We're going to
Nan's to supper,' he heard her say.

'Yes, I know, you told me.' He finished fastening
his gloves, pressing down the little brown studs on the
inside of his wrists. 'Give her my love. I'll wait up for
you, and you can give me all their news.' He closed
the window, nodding a terse goodbye.

Charis waited until he had managed to join the
main traffic stream. She could see him sitting straight
behind the wheel. Her father's life hadn't been easy,
she knew that from Nan. He had lost two wives—the
first, Nan's mother, in a riding accident, while the
second, her own mother, had died when she was born.
Nan, at that time newly married, had learned that she
couldn't have children; she and Harold had brought
up Charis as their own. Her father had evinced little

interest in her till she started her nurse's training, when he had suddenly wanted to see much more of her. It was he who had introduced her to Neil, a year and a half ago, he who had been so pleased when they got engaged. He was a difficult man in many ways, difficult to get near, his secretiveness made a barrier like a wall. But still, we *are* drawing closer now, which has to be good news, Charis thought as she turned away from the kerb.

Hanson's office building was a flat-fronted Georgian house, set between two similar houses, occupied by a dental group, and a firm of solicitors called Mathieson & Pratt. Hansons' front door was open, but most of the staff had gone home. One or two stragglers waved to Charis as they ran down the steps, scarves and collars pulled up round their ears. Two of the partners were still upstairs, while in his ground floor office Neil Chambers was signing his letters and doing them up himself. He had joined the firm two years ago, he sold houses and flats, did surveys and valuations when required. Knowing better than to interrupt him, Charis turned to the waiting-room. She would intercept him when he came out, he would expect her to be there. She had quite forgotten that her father had told her Neil had a caller. She saw him at once as she opened the door. He had his back to her, he was wearing the sheepskin jacket that she had stared at in the store. Even before he swung round she knew who it was . . . Guy Morland. Guy Morland *again!* What on earth was he doing here? Taken aback, taken off guard, she uttered the very first thing that came into her head.

'I've not followed you here,' she said.

'I didn't really suppose even you would go to those lengths!' He gave a short laugh, but her own surprise was reflected on his face. He was quickly in command of the situation. 'No doubt, like me,' he added, 'you're here on business, so why not come in and sit down?'

What she wanted to do more than anything else was step backwards and wait in the hall, but that would be ridiculous. In no way would she give him the satisfaction of seeing how his presence affected her. She sat down on a hard upright chair—easy for springing up from. She unbelted her coat, while he seated himself behind the central table. She heard the rustle of a newspaper, the flick it made as he shook it. A fleeting glance confirmed that he was screened from her view; all she could see was his hands and part of his sleeve. But why, she wondered, was he waiting for Neil? Why did he want to see him? Then she felt she knew. He was here on business, he would want somewhere to live when he took up his post at the end of January. He could apply to the hospital for residency, but most Registrars preferred to live out, and have a pad of their own. Also, of course, he might be married, he might have children. Was he married? As she glanced again at the paper barricade, he lowered it, closed it and put it down.

'Are you house-hunting too?' he asked, thereby seeming to prove that her guess about him was absolutely right.

'I'm not here on business, I've called for Neil . . . Neil Chambers, my fiancé. I think you're waiting to see him.'

'Yes, I am, but how could you know?' He snapped the question and his brows rose up.

'My father told me,' she said. 'Father's the senior partner here, I've just seen him leaving.'

'I see,' but he still looked mystified.

'Our name is Littleton. The Hansons died off years ago, but the firm's name was retained.'

'I think firms' names usually are, and this one seems well known. Sir Rodney suggested I should come here. I rang through and spoke to a secretary, who made no bones about the appointment, even though it was late.'

'Sir Rodney's name opens, or keeps open, most of the doors in Seftonbridge,' said Charis with a touch of acid, jerking her chin at him. She had gained, she felt, a kind of ascendancy, she felt she had the advantage—a mean one, perhaps—but here at Hansons, here in her father's office, she was on her home ground, more or less, and he *had* got a hell of a nerve, strolling round at this time of evening, asking to see Neil, making him late . . . even later than he was. 'Have you far to travel this evening?' She fixed him with her eye.

'Back home, you mean?' His gaze was unwavering.

'Yes, that's what I mean.'

'I'm from Warminster, in Wiltshire, but I'm not travelling back tonight. I'm spending the weekend here in Seftonbridge.' He supplied the information with courteous readiness, yet somehow managed, by tone and expression, a glint in those slate grey eyes, to convey the word 'Satisfied?' at the end.

There was no talk for some time after that; there was just the sound of the clock—a stately grandfather tocking away in its corner by the window, and the rush and pelt and blare of the traffic outside. 'Are you orthopaedic trained?' he asked, as she unzipped her bag and took out the latest Ellis Rand paperback.

'I am, yes. I took a post-registration course in Oxfordshire. I got my Orthopaedic Nursing Certificate, staffed in Oxford for a time, then came to Seftonbridge. I've been here just a year.'

'Where did you do your general training?'

'At St Mildred's, London Bridge.'

'A very good stable . . . they turn out the best.'

I'm a good nurse, she wanted to say. Charis wasn't vain, but she did not believe in underrating herself. Confidence in nursing was vitally important. How terrible for the patients if they felt that their care was in nervous, uncertain hands.

'Orthopaedic nurses,' said Guy Morland, 'aren't all that thick on the ground.'

'Yes, well, that's the way it goes,' Charis replied, moving a strand of silken hair back behind her ear. As she did so the diamond cluster ring on her engagement finger winked in the light and caught the eye of the man behind the table. The ring could never be worn on the ward, it had to be kept in her handbag, in the hessian bag that her father so deplored.

'Do you intend to nurse after marriage?' he asked.

'I hope to, for a time.' He wanted to know an awful lot. What a catechism this was! She was saved further questions by the opening of the door, and by Neil coming into the room. His glance passed from Charis to Guy Morland; he addressed the latter first.

'Mr Morland?'

'Yes.'

'I'm Neil Chambers.' He smiled and looked welcoming. He was tall and fair, and broadly built, his eyes a clear light blue; he wore spectacles with very pale frames, which gave him a foreign look. Charis, who was partly Greek, looked English to the last eyelash, with her pink pearl skin and turned-up nose. Neil and I are impostors both, she thought with a burst of affection, and a long look at both men as they stood shaking hands.

'Au revoir, Miss Littleton,' said Guy Morland, bowing on his way to the door.

Neil looked surprised. 'So you've met Charis?'

'Not until today.' Guy Morland's gaze fixed itself on the wall behind Charis's head. Unaware of any undercurrents, Neil slammed the heel of his hand against his forehead,

'But of course, of course . . . you're from the hospital! I remember my secretary saying so. She just told me in passing, though. Oh Friday nights, office staff like to get off early. Not that I blame them, not at all.' He flicked a glance at his watch.

'Rest assured I shan't keep you long . . . a matter of minutes only,' said Guy Morland, as he followed Neil out of the room.

He was a quarter of an hour exactly—Charis sat timing him. She heard him come out of Neil's room, heard the two of them cross the hall. They had a brief conversation at the front door, then Neil came in to her. Within minutes they were on their way to Nan's.

'He wants a flat,' he told her, as he drove with his usual care through the thick of the traffic in the shopping part of the town. 'Later he'll be looking for a house and garden, which rather made me wonder if he, like us, is getting married soon.'

'Perhaps,' she suggested, 'he's married now.'

'No, he's not—he told me that. He stated his requirements very precisely, much to my relief. For a medical man he was very businesslike.'

'Medical men aren't fools, Neil!'

'No, of course not. I didn't mean that.' He gave her a quick, troubled glance, then switched on the radio. 'Let's have some music, shall we?' The strains of a Chopin nocturne filled the car as it turned down Regent Street.

Charis was as fond of music as Neil, it was one of the interests they shared, but this evening she couldn't enjoy it; the sound flowed into her ears and out again, leaving no soothing trail. She stared out at the teeming streets, at the cavalcade of lights, gleaming and dipping, swaying on bicycles, streaming from shop windows, shining more softly from college gates and walls. It was some time before they were clear of the town, and neither spoke very much till the traffic lay well behind them, and the spire of Luffham Church, at the turn-off point to Little Molding, came eerily out of the mist.

'As luck would have it,' Neil made the turn, 'he may be able to rent Dr Leigh Stanton's flat, I thought of that at once. Stanton's recently moved to a house

in Lawns Road, his wife's expecting a child. He wants
to let the flat furnished for six or eight months, he
said. It's Mayfield Court, College Walk. Morland took
the particulars. While he was with me I rang Margaret
Brodie—she lives there, as you know. She agreed to
get the key from the office and show him over the flat
tomorrow morning. She's always helpful, never makes
a fuss. I suppose it was rather a cheek to ask her, but
as she's right on the spot, and as it's our weekend off,
and we seldom get one together, I took a chance. I
hope your father won't mind.'

'I don't suppose she'll tell him' said Charis,
'Margaret's discretion itself.'

Miss Brodie was Cedric Littleton's secretary—a
pleasant, efficient woman in her mid-thirties, whom
everyone liked, but nevertheless dubbed spineless. She
allowed people, Cedric especially, to put on her far
too much. She was fiercely loyal to her employer, but
she wouldn't tittle-tattle, nor carry tales, just for the
sake of it. She liked Neil and considered him a great
asset to the firm. She lived at number eight Mayfield
Court, a purpose-built block of flats which overlooked
the river and the lock.

'If he likes the flat,' Neil went on, 'he'll give me a
ring on Monday. My view is it's just right for him,
not too far from the Hospital, but restful and quiet,
practically countrified.'

'Yes,' said Charis, 'I'm sure you're right.' She
glanced at Neil and smiled. From the look on his face
she knew he wasn't talking to her so much as giving
adequate rein to his thoughts. Neil liked his plans to
be watertight, he liked to be sure they were sound; he
was cautious by nature, and mindful of snags, and he
never, but never, *never* left anything to chance.

She was glad he didn't, because she knew her own
faults. She was too impulsive by far, and she needed
a slice of Neil's natural caution to act as a kind of
brake. There were times, though, when she wouldn't

have minded him being a little rash, but then if he were different in one way, he might be different in others, and that would be awful, as he wouldn't be Neil, not the Neil she looked up to and loved. You can't divide people up into pieces and take out the scraps or snippets that you don't like, and expect them to join up the same.

'How are we going to spend our two days?' he asked her, changing the subject. For the rest of the journey out to Nan's they discussed their weekend plans. Charis had been going to tell him about the incident in Carter & Mayhew's store, but in the end she kept her own counsel, she didn't want to discuss it, not even with Neil. What she felt she must do was bury it good and deep, and start afresh as though it had never occurred.

CHAPTER TWO

WHEN Guy Morland took up his post at the end of January there was a new set of patients in Athelstone, apart from William Ivyson, the spinal case, and Paul Dobson with his knee.

Sister Holt, small, grey-haired and prim, wearing her purple dress just a shade too long, greeted him at the doors. Rob Peele was with him; Sir Rodney was in Theatre, starting on his list. Charis, busy with dressings, was removing the sutures from the wound of a patient with a fractured tibia. Part of her job was to teach the learners, and she had Nurse Adams with her. Jane Adams was in her first year; she was nervous, but anxious to learn. Charis explained that the fracture had occurred at the rounded end of the bone and was called a tibial table (condyle) break.

She was fully aware, as she took up the forceps and scissors from the trolley, that Guy Morland was in the ward, for she had heard Sister greet him, had heard them talking as they walked to the central desk. She and Nurse Adams were concealed by the curtains pulled round the patient's bed. But imagine him coming before ten a.m., imagine not warning Sister! How awful to be caught in the middle of a dressing. Oh well, it couldn't be helped. Still hearing their voices, Charis went on with her task.

The patient, Mr Tovey, enjoyed being practised on. It wasn't every day he had two young women dancing attendance on him. Both of them wore overalls. The elder one, Staff Nurse Littleton, drew out the stitches, he hardly felt a thing. 'All right, Mr Tovey?' she asked him, eyes smiling over her mask. He assured her he was champion, because things were moving at last. His long leg plaster had been taken off yesterday, and very good it was not to feel he was in an iron cast.

George Tovey hailed from Yorkshire. He had injured his leg while on a visit to his youngest daughter, who lived in Seftonbridge. He had stumbled down her patio steps, a daft thing to do, especially for a man still in his prime.

Charis was gently cleaning his leg, when the curtains were whisked aside to show Sister first, looking pint-sized, with Guy Morland towering behind her, so close that one got the impression she was imprinted on his white coat. Rob was somewhere behind Guy Morland, Charis could see his sleeve. She put down the forceps, and Nurse Adams, who looked to her for guidance, was told by Sister to help out in the sluice. She went off quickly, glad to do so, while Charis moved the trolley to make way for Guy Morland who was edging round to her side.

'May I see before you cover up, Staff?' Once again she found herself caught in that penetrating gaze of his; once again she longed to escape.

'Yes, Mr Morland.' She took a step backwards, ballooning out the curtains, feeling them sift against the wings of her cap.

He spoke to the patient, put him at ease, then bent to look at the leg. He forbore to touch it, but his eyes missed nothing. 'Looks fine,' he straightened up. 'Skin nice and healthy . . . may I see the notes?' Sister produced them and he scanned the details. "Large condylar fragment, immobilised by internal screw, long leg plaster." 'When did the plaster come off?' he asked; he was trying to turn the page.

'Yesterday, sir,' Mr Tovey spoke first.

Guy Morland smiled. 'You'll be glad about that.'

'I'll be glad to be out of here, sir—no offence, you understand.'

'None taken,' Guy Morland assured him, 'but these things can't be hurried. The next stage is knee mobilising exercises, then if all goes well, we'll get you standing, with the aid of crutches, and go on from there. You'll be able to put more weight on your leg, as each day passes—progressively, but *gradually,* it's a stage that can't be rushed.'

Mr Tovey puffed out his cheeks. 'I know you'll do your best. 'Twas my fault for falling—ought to have had more sense!'

'Accidents *will* happen, Mr Tovey.' Guy Morland touched his shoulder. 'Right, Staff,' he nodded at Charis, 'we'll leave you in peace.' He stepped back, and Charis moved into his place. There was just the bandaging now, and the cradle, and getting the bed put straight.

'When you've finished,' Sister put in crisply, 'perhaps you would see to the pharmacist. He's in my office, waiting to check the drugs.'

'I'll do that next,' said Charis, reaching for the trolley. Rob nudged her as he moved off in Sister's and Guy Morland's wake. 'So far so good,' he grinned. Charis shut him out, whisking the curtains, glad to be on her own.

Having made Mr Tovey comfortable, and got out of her overall, she made her way to Sister's office, producing the drugs cupboard keys, and the registers for Mr Gee, one of the pharmacists. It was his job to check the ward stock of drugs every three months. It was a painstaking and tedious chore—every ampoule, capsule and tablet, every bottle level had to be checked against what had been given out. By the time he had finished and had his coffee, Guy Morland and Rob had completed their round and left the ward, and Sister Holt was immersed in an argument with the Catering Manager.

Over lunch in the nurses' dining-room, some two hours later, Charis and Dilys Hughes, a staff nurse from Docherty Ward, caught up on all their respective news. Dilys raved about Guy Morland. 'He's really quite something, Charis! Sister was off this morning, so I had to do the honours. Oh, how I love tall, dark, handsome men, and Morland's got the lot! He's so elegant, isn't he, so distinguished . . . and have you noticed his *hands!*'

Charis had, so she merely nodded, letting her friend rattle on. Dily's language, well peppered with adjectives, was the way she always talked. 'And he's not married, either,' she continued, 'I got that from Sharon Farr—you know, the clerk in Admin; she dealt with the applications. He's thirty-three and a half, and he's got specialist qualifications. Of course, Sharon shouldn't have told me, really.'

'You're telling me she shouldn't!' Charis began to tackle her pudding, a banana and custard mash with ice-cream on top, which tasted, thank heaven, much better than it looked. She wondered if Guy Morland realised what interest he had aroused. He most likely did. He was probably amused.

'And he's living in Dr Stanton's flat,' she heard Dilys say.

'Actually, Dil, I knew that. Neil did all the arranging.'

'You never said!'

'I suppose I forgot.' Charis said absently. Neil had been amazed that Guy Morland hadn't quibbled about the rent. 'Is he well-heeled, do you think, darling, or do Senior Registrars get paid right over the top these days?' Those had been his words. Charis had laughed and said she had no idea. Neil had a high regard for money. His father, now retired, had been a merchant banker, and some of his expertise, even wizardry, where finance was concerned, had rubbed off on Neil . . . at least that was what Charis always supposed.

'You're very quiet, Charis.' Dilys's voice filtered

through. 'You look worried too. Are you okay?'

'Absolutely fine!'

'Love life all right?'

'Not a cloud is sight, unlike that lot out there.' Charis nodded towards the line of windows, past which snowflakes twirled and whirled in a frenzied sideways dance. 'I don't like the winter much.'

'It's your Latin blood objecting!' Dilys knew that Charis's mother had been half Greek; she also knew she had died in the Seftonbridge General, giving birth to her, twenty-four years ago. 'But talking of the Stantons,' she went on, pulling her coffee towards her, 'they're giving a housewarming party at the end of February.'

'I know they are.'

'Rose Cleeve told me,' (Dilys's informants were legion) 'she and her husband have been invited, as she works on Women's Med. Mrs Stanton was once the Sister, you know. She and Leigh Stanton had a whirl-wind romance and ended up married, about two years ago. He's rather nice—attractive too, in a racy kind of way. She's more quiet, sort of serene, but she's obviously got what it takes. I'm still waiting for an eligible Registrar to fall for me.' Dilys looked rueful, she wished she could lose some weight.

'As a matter of fact,' said Charis, 'Neil and I have been invited. I rather think Dr Stanton asked Neil because of the business connection. My father has been asked because he plays golf with Mrs Stanton's father, and Nan and Harold are going because they landscaped their garden. I think the idea is to thank everyone who helped them settled in.'

'Some people get all the luck!' Dilys was plainly envious.

'I've only been asked because of Neil . . . I mean, because we're engaged. I hardly know the Stantons. I'm not all that keen on going,' Charis was at pains to try to explain.

'Do you good, be a super evening . . . you'll have a fantastic time, and you never know,' a gleam of mischief appeared in Dilys's eye, 'Leigh Stanton may ask Guy Morland, he being a tenant of his.'

Charis rose to the bait. 'Oh no, surely not!'

'Well, don't look so horrified. What's he ever done to you?'

'Not a single thing.'

'Too bad! Now, that's really tough!' Dilys might have teased on, if two nurses from Gynae hadn't joined them at their table, when the talk veered to the finals of the squash tournament due to be played in the Social Club that night.

Guy Morland was in the ward most days during the next three weeks, sometimes with Sir Rodney, sometimes on his own, sometimes with a bevy of medics in close and rapt attendance. His theatre list was as long as Sir Rodney's. Rob was very impressed. 'He can be sharp, snap your head off at times . . . he's not easy-going,' he said, 'but I've learned quite a bit from him, Charis; he takes the trouble to teach.'

'I'm glad you're pleased,' said Charis, with her eye on Mr Ivyson. Nurses Barford and Adams were washing his hair. They had removed the head of his bed; the bowl of water took the place of his pillow, and Nurse Adams was supporting his neck. There was a smell of shampoo, and a good deal of laughter and chat.

'It gets more like a beauty parlour in here every single day!' remarked Mr Ivyson, as he stared straight up at Jane Adams' pretty face. He was popular with the nurses, he was almost a model patient, but as he said, he had little scope in which to get up to tricks. 'Just you wait till I'm out of my turtle's shell!' he warned.

'Don't you like him, Charis?' Rob enquired.

'I suppose you mean G.M.?' She brought her attention back to the young houseman at her side. 'I've not really had much to do with him. Sister copes with him mostly.'

'Never fear, your turn will come!' said Rob with a grin, as he rushed off, coat flapping, to Docherty Ward.

Her turn came next day when Guy Morland visited Mr Galleon, whose long leg plaster was giving trouble, chafing his toes and groin. Mr Galleon was a retired butcher, with a lively imagination. He dreamed of bones, all of them shattered, and spent his waking hours visualising his own shinbone, no longer in whole condition, and he hated the thought; he longed to be perfect again.

'All I want you to do is reassure him, while I get to work with this,' Guy Morland explained to Charis, as he brought the electric saw out of the plaster room during the afternoon. Sister was engaged with the relative of a patient and would probably be some time. Charis plugged in the saw by Mr Galleon's bed.

'It'll make a shocking noise,' she warned him, 'but that's nothing to worry about. It's a vibrating instrument, it oscillates, and it can't cut *you,* only the plaster, it's geared to do just that thing.'

'Doesn't look much like a saw to me, more like some kind of gun,' he remarked, as she laid a plastic sheet over the bed.

'Now, what I'm going to do, Mr Galleon,' Guy Morland broke in, 'is take a little of this plaster from off the top of your toes. It catches them, doesn't it, you told me so, and I can see where it's been chafing. Then we'll take a little bit off the thigh end, make you more comfortable.'

'It's a rum kind of saw,' Mr Galleon insisted, watching the rotary blade begin to spin and whirr, as Charis switched the current on.

'I'm starting at the toe end . . . here we go.' Guy Morland bent to his task. As the instrument engaged the plaster a high-pitched KARRR-ing sound shivered the air, while fragments of plaster rattled down on to the sheet. Mr Galleon, once he dared open his eyes, could see far more of his toes. 'Well, go on, wriggle them . . . see how they feel,' Guy smiled at him.

'Much better, sir . . . got more space, feel more airy, like.' A powdery mist hung over his leg, and we ought, Charis thought, to have done all this in the plaster room. Sister will have a fit!

'Fine, now I'm coming up here.' Guy moved to the top of his leg. The harsh KARRRrrr of the saw came again, this time for slightly longer. The old man's hand gripped Charis's, he felt his head would split, as well as his plaster. 'All done—good man!' Guy smoothed the edge. 'We'll have you in a walking plaster very soon, you know with the foot part reinforced and a zimmer heel applied.'

'I'll be good as new, won't I?' Mr Galleon's face relaxed.

'Probably better,' teased Guy; he and Charis left the ward, he carrying the saw—and yes, it did look a bit like a gun. He could have been a hijacker of wards, and she his willing accomplice, or unwilling hostage. Charis stifled a laugh.

Standing outside the ward doors, Guy thanked her for her help. 'I did nothing,' she protested, but he shook his head at that.

'Untrue, Staff Nurse! Our Mr Galleon felt better for having you there. We all need our hand held, need reassuring at times.'

'Why, yes,' she agreed, 'I suppose we do.' She smiled up at him, his approval pleasing her out of all proportion to the actual words he used. I shall be able to work with him perfectly easily when the need arises, she thought. It's not necessary to like him as a man, just respect him as a surgeon, and that I can do, perfectly easily.

Dilys's comment that Guy might be at the Stantons' housewarming party was borne out in fact. Charis

saw him as soon as she entered the room. There he
stood, glass in hand, svelte and smooth as ever, dark
head bent to the woman at his side. The woman was
Sister Tolbie from Orthopaedic Theatres. She and Guy
were talking to Sister Hammond from Women's
Medical, and the consultant, Professor Selby, and his
wife.

Charis was with Neil and her father, and his secretary, Margaret Brodie. Margaret had been only too
pleased to partner her employer. She admired him,
was fond of him . . . too fond, perhaps . . . but
no one knew that, least of all him. Margaret was
adept at keeping her feelings under wraps. She and
Cedric made their way to the bar, while Charis and
Neil joined Nancy and Harold on the other side of
the room.

Parties weren't Harold Roffey's scene, but Nan had
made him come. 'We can't possibly *not* go,
Harold . . . you know you like the Stantons. We
needn't stay long, but we must at least put in an
appearance.' So here they were—Nan, tall and
rawboned, in a dress she had tried to lengthen, but
not pressed properly; it still bore the mark of the hem.
Harold was beside her, small and wiry, brown, and
navy-suited, setting his mouth in a smile so determined
that it made his muscles ache. When he caught sight
of Charis the smile changed gear, became beaming
and genuine. As they joined forces, Harold began to
relax.

Charis and Nan had their father's eyes, green-hazel
and thickly lashed. At that moment Nan's were fixed
on Guy Morland. 'We've been introduced,' she told
Charis. 'I had no idea he looked like that . . . you
might have told me, Charis.'

'Charis is dying to sketch him,' chuckled Neil, and
Nan said she wasn't surprised. Charis had a flair,
more than that, a talent, for making lightning sketches
of people she knew, of faces that caught her eye and

imagination. Sometimes she did them in caricature, which was therapeutic and fun—for her, that was—but it had its dangerous side.

'What about the girl? She came with him, but I didn't catch her name?' asked Nan, bending her russet head to Charis's golden one.

'She's our Orthopaedic Theatre Sister. She'll meet him practically daily, when he operates, I mean. She'll know his techniques, keep things running smoothly. She's very attractive, I expect they've got friendly.'

'Over the bones and gore!' laughed Neil, and Nan shuddered. Charis shut him up.

She would hardly have known Sister Tolbie tonight. Black pants with a vividly striped satin top was a very far cry indeed from the starkness of a theatre gown and mask.

More guests were arriving, but the house stretched itself well. It was spacious and open-plan, which allowed for moving around. Tawny and gold chrysanthemums in rough pottery urns glowed in corners, spicing the air; they came from Roffey's Nurseries, Nan had delivered them only the day before. 'It's a lovely house,' said Charis, as Leigh and Kate Stanton, their host and hostess, came to talk to them.

'We have your fiancé to thank for that,' Kate Stanton smiled, 'he pointed out its potential, got us interested.'

'Neil,' Cedric Littleton remarked, moving up behind them, 'can tell a good house from a bad one by instinct, *and* what's more, he can sell both types if he gives his mind to it!' They all laughed, and Neil looked pleased, while Cedric, with Margaret in tow, went off to talk to his golfing friend, Charles Holmes.

The evening was well over halfway through before Charis and Guy met. Charis had gone to tidy her hair, and when she came downstairs Neil was talking to Joanne Tolbie over by the buffet table. Guy and a thin little man whose name was Fergus Pendle were standing together at the bottom of the stairs. Mr Pendle moved off to find his wife, which left Charis and Guy with a clear space between them; they could hardly not converge.

'Can I get you a drink, something to eat?' He was very solicitous.

She shook her head. 'No, thanks,' she said, 'I've just about had my fill.'

'Mind if I finish this?' Guy had a glass of Scotch in his hand.

'Of course not.' She felt the touch of his hand as he moved her out of the way of a passing group of medical students. One of them yelled: 'Hi, Charis!' They were full of good cheer, plainly enjoying themselves.

'You have an unusual name,' remarked Guy, as they found two vacant chairs and sat down under the slope of the stairs.

'It was my mother's name, she was half Greek, and she died when I was born. My grandmother, my mother's mother, was married to a Greek doctor. She was a nurse at St Mildred's, London Bridge. Her home is in Athens now. She runs a private orthopaedic clinic just off Syntagma Square.'

'Have you been there?' Guy enquired.

'I have, yes, several times. And Helen, my grandmother, comes over here every year. She's widowed now, but I don't think she'll ever return to England for good.'

'Interesting . . . and an interesting name, Charis,' he pronounced it slowly, rather as though he liked it, while his grey eyes appraised her over the rim of his glass. Her hair was down this evening; released from its customary pleat, it curtained her face and lay richly soft against the cream of her dress. Her eyes held dreams, her head had a tilt, the lines of her body were poetry. She suited her name, her Greek name meaning grace. 'When are you getting married?' he asked, so suddenly and abruptly that she stared at him feeling momentarily floored. 'Perhaps it's a state secret,' he prompted.

She laughed and shook back her hair. 'No, not a secret, just undecided, but it's likely to be in August. As soon as negotiations for Hansons' new branch are concluded, we can make firm plans. Neil will be a partner then.'

'Will he, indeed?'

She disliked his tone. 'He's more than earned it,' she flashed.

'I'm sure he has, I don't doubt it.' There was silence and then he said, 'So there'll be another Hansons' office here in Seftonbridge?'

'In Kingsford,' she corrected.

'Kingsford?' His brows went up.

'Yes, forty miles east of here, it's not all that far from the coast. We're very much looking forward to it. If all goes as planned, I'll be leaving the General Hospital in July.'

'You sound as though you can hardly wait!'

'I shall miss everyone here—the hospital *and* the town.' It seemed polite to add that. But she meant it too, there was truth in her words, for in her heart of hearts she knew she wished Neil could stay at the office in Princes Parade. She loved the town, loved its buildings, its river and its bridges, its emerald lawns, its famous Backs, its dipping willow trees. She loved the hustle and bustle, and bells, and loved its tranquillity. Seftonbridge was a town of contrasts, and she felt at one with it; she always had, even as a child. 'I hope to get a nursing post at Kingsford Royal Infirmary,' she told Guy, lacing her hands in her lap.

'You'll have no trouble.' He uncrossed his legs and leaned back in the small winged chair. He looked exceedingly cheerful, she noticed, stealing a glance at him. He wasn't bothering with pleasantries, he wasn't bothering to say—even if he didn't mean it—that he'd be sorry to see her go. 'Whereabouts in Kingsford will the office be?' he asked conversationally. 'I know the town slightly, I've driven through it on my way to Felixstowe.'

'It's right in the main shopping street, opposite a branch of Carter & Mayhew's department store. My father felt it was . . . felt it was . . . such . . . a good . . . position.' Her voice faltered and died, eddied away like drifty smoke, while the words 'Carter & Mayhew' wrote themselves a foot high in the air in blazing letters of fire, scorching her face, shrivelling her body, reminding her of that day, that awful day when she'd taken him for a thief.

He was remembering it too, of that she had no doubt at all. The space between their two chairs took on a life of its own. She felt rather than saw him move, heard him clearing his throat, and she held her breath, praying hard; perhaps he was going to say, 'Let's forget about it, shall we?' or 'Water under the bridge', or even, 'You did what you thought was right, don't worry any more'. Perhaps he was, but if so, he was taking his time about it. He was moving too, getting up; she could hear the slithery sound of his chair legs on the polished woodblock floor. 'Our partners are about to join us,' he said above her head. Looking across the room, she saw Neil and Joanne Tolbie, with Margaret Brodie, bearing down on them.

She was scarcely aware of the small-talk that went on after that. She supposed she contributed to it, she was aware of Joanne Tolbie saying how very much she liked her dress. This was just prior to Joanne and Guy being whisked off by the Stantons to see a variety of orchid in their new conservatory.

Margaret Brodie was fussing about Cedric Littleton, who had gone to fetch his coat. He was tired, and bored, and tetchy, and he wanted nothing more than to get back to the quiet of his home. 'We might as well push off ourselves, don't you think?' Neil said to

Charis, who agreed at once, only too readily.

They all four left together, walking the short distance from Lawns Road to College Walk, seeing Margaret into her flat on the first floor of Mayfield Court, where Guy Morland also lived. His flat was on the second floor—Charis cast her eyes upward. It would command an unrivalled view of the river right up to the lock. His windows were in darkness, but they would be, of course; he was still at the Stantons' party. She drew a quick breath, then let it out, seeing it vaporize and mingle with Neil's, who had his arm round her waist. It was good to walk close, the night was bitter, there was rime on the bordering trees; their branches rattled woodenly in the spears of freezing wind driving in over the outlying Fens.

Neil lived in digs, very comfortable ones, on the other side of town. He had left his car at Cranleigh, Cedric Littleton's house, and Charis's home. They were nearing its driveway now. Timbered and gabled, and mock-Tudor, it stood on its own plot of ground. The rooms were large and tastefully furnished, the windows mullioned. Charis loved it, and so did Cedric, who had lived there since his first marriage—not that he cared a fig for memories, he never looked over his shoulder, never looked back; he believed in pressing on. He employed a daily housekeeper, who also tended the garden and exercised Homer, his noble red setter. Homer's greeting was rapturous, as they let themselves into the hall. His beanbag was there, this was his 'station', and he never deserted it on the rare occasions when he was left alone. He followed his master upstairs to his room; there was a television programme on land values that Cedric wanted to see. But even more than that he wanted to stretch himself out on his bed. He was tired, and his limbs felt leaden. He was in his seventieth year—not old, perhaps, but not young either, hardly the first flush of youth. He grunted as he bent to unlace his shoes.

Down in the sitting-room Charis removed the guard from the open fire. She piled on fresh logs, which quickly caught, making shapes and shadows and warmth, filling the room with the scent of apple wood. Log fires were romantic. She sat on the couch, her head on Neil's shoulder, and his arm came round her, drawing her closer still. 'It won't be so very long now,' he said, 'before we have our own home.'

'Five months plus!'

'It'll soon go.' He tipped her face to his. He kissed her and she responded, aware of the warmth of the room, the faint mumble of her father's television over their heads, the short, sharp bark of a dog outside. Neil's lovemaking didn't whirl her away, didn't raise her to the heights, but it made feel loved and cherished, and the feeling they each of them had, one for the other, would last for ever, she had thought when they got engaged. She still thought so—well, of course she did. She opened her eyes, seeing in close-up the grain of Neil's skin, his whole face as they drew apart, with its blunt clean features and cleft chin.

'It wasn't a bad party, was it?' she said.

'No, not bad at all.' They settled down to talk about it, just like a married couple . . . an old married couple. Charis gazed into the fire.

'I noticed you chatting up Sister Tolbie,' she said in mock reproof.

'It was the other way round,' Neil smiled selfconsciously, not entirely displeased. 'She swooped on me, talked away nineteen to the dozen.'

'She's attractive.'

'I agree, she is, if one's taste runs to smouldering types. Mine doesn't, and *her* taste is plainly for dark smouldering men. She's an old friend of Morland's. Did you know that, Charis? She met him years ago, when they were both at one of the London hospitals . . . the Walbrook, I think she said.'

'No, I didn't know.' Charis sounded stifled, and he

moved to give her more room.

'She might be the reason, or one of them, why he came to Seftonbridge.'

'That's very possible,' Charis said slowly, 'but it's none of our business, is it?'

'Of course not, no.' Neil jumped up as a flake of burning wood spat out on to the hearthrug. 'Dangerous things, log fires,' he muttered, replacing the wire guard. The romantic leaping life of the fire became quenched behind the mesh. Charis felt a sinking of her own spirits, and a shaft of annoyance as well. The last thing she wanted to speculate on was Guy Morland's love life. So when Neil returned to her side, after carefully inspecting the rug, she changed the subject and talked about Hansons, which interested them both. It was then that she thought to ask him, threading her arm through his, who would work for her father when Margaret went off on holiday—a long holiday, five weeks of it, because she hadn't had one last year. She was spending it with her parents in Aberdeen.

'My own girl's got to double up, do both jobs,' he told her. 'Still, she's very conscientious, and I don't doubt that she'll cope. Margaret has earned her holiday,' he added generously, 'she takes a tremendous load of worry off Cedric's shoulders, you know.'

'She always looks terribly worried. How old do you think she is?'

'She's thirty-four, she told me once. I don't know how it came up. She looks older than that, doesn't she?' Neil's shoulders rose in a shrug. It astounds me that she never married—she's not bad-looking, she's capable too, she would never let anyone down.'

'She might *still* marry . . . she's hardly past it, not at thirty-four!'

'She's wedded to Hansons,' said Neil, and Charis agreed with him. Everyone had to find their own niche, and perhaps that was Margaret's. She had been with her father over fourteen years.

Their talk veered from Margaret to houses, and the sort they would have when they married. Neither wanted anything ultra-modern. 'Something like this would be perfect,' said Neil, just as Homer, adept at opening doors, let himself in and laid his domed head in the middle of Charis's lap. His arrival meant that her father must have put out his light. As soon as this happened Homer knew he had to make tracks for the hall; he wasn't allowed to sleep on the upper floor.

'I ought to be going,' she heard Neil say. She went out with him to the car, an anorak slung over her shoulders, and half her attention on Homer who was swinging his fringed legs over the frosty lawn. 'Goodnight, then, darling.' Neil bent and kissed her. 'Hurry up and go back in the warm.' He slammed himself into the car and drove off. He had turned it to face the gates before they left for the party earlier that evening. A little forethought saves time and trouble, was one of the Neil's axioms. And of course he was right, he nearly always was.

Charis waited to hear the brief pip of his horn, which meant he was in the lane, then she called Homer and went thoughtfully into the house.

CHAPTER THREE

THE weather decided to warm up during the third week in March. Daffodils turned the green of the Backs to a carpet of moving gold. Tabby-coloured ducklings followed their flat-bottomed mothers across a river expanse that was looking-glass.

Charis, cycling the short distance from Cranleigh House to the hospital, had discarded her coat for her scarlet-lined cloak . . . how marvellous to think it wouldn't be winter again for seven months! And springtime in Seftonbridge was magic. She lifted her face to a breeze that smelled of the river, of trees and damp earth, of ancient cloistered buildings, of sun-warmed parapets and paths. But traffic fumes predominated once she reached Princes Parade, and entered the Hospital precinct by the side gates.

She had been on days off, a long weekend, and today she was on lates—the shift between one p.m. and nine o'clock at night. Lifting her bicycle into the stands at the rear of the laundry buildings, she crossed the yard and went up to the Ortho floor. Sister Holt, all set to go off duty, was waiting to give the report. She did so quietly, sitting at the Nurses' Station. There had been two admissions the day before, and young Paul Dobson was being discharged at two o'clock, just prior to visiting time. 'His brother Martin is coming for him.' Sister replaced the Kardex. 'Mr Morland very kindly said he would try to get up to see Paul mainly to say goodbye, but also, I strongly suspect, to try to instil some common sense into that foolish young man.' She clicked her tongue, and her small neat bosom heaved with the depth of her sigh. Charis knew what she meant, and how she felt, and she fully sympathised. Shortly after Christmas, a mere three weeks before he was due for discharge, Paul, on his way to the bathrooms, had decided to disobey orders and do an unauthorised recce down the length of the corridor. He had lost his balance and in lurching to regain it had damaged his knee, rupturing the repaired tendon all over again. This had necessitated further surgery, and Sir Rodney had blown his top. 'Wasting my time . . . Daft thing to do . . . Setting yourself back . . . Don't you young people *ever* do what you are told?' And if that were not enough, poor Paul had contracted a chest infection. In all he had been in hospital fourteen weeks. But today . . . oh yes, today, today he was going home. In another half an hour or so his twin brother Martin would be here to collect him; he felt he could hardly wait.

As soon as Sister Holt had gone off, Charis made a point of talking to the new patients whom she had not met before. Mr Clover, in his late thirties, was in for osteotomy, to correct the deformity of his left hip, due to osteo arthritis. Mr Renner, in the same age group, was having a knee operation to remove a loose body from the joint. Both men were on Thursday's theatre list, their beds were adjacent. Fortunately they gave every appearance of getting on well together, which would help them during their stay in hospital.

Paul was playing Scrabble with Mr Galleon in the day room, a small room with sliding doors at the far end of the ward. 'I can't keep my mind on it, Staff,' he said, as Charis went in to see him. He looked matchstick-thin in his skin-tight jeans and loose battle-dress jacket. His orange hair, which seemed to grow straight out of the top of his head, glowed like a beacon, so did his nose; the rest of his face was pale. His elbow crutch was within reach, and he grabbed it and got to his feet, as he saw his brother come through the main ward doors. 'Here he is! Good old Mart, trust him to be on time!'

Charis turned to speak to Martin, who was dressed the same as Paul. They were identical twins, and seeing them together was like having double vision. Charis suggested that Paul didn't go, not for a minute or two. 'Better hang on until two o'clock, Paul. Mr Morland wants to see you, he's coming up especially, so you can't just take yourself off.'

'All right, if you say so.' Paul looked truculent.

'I do.' She made her voice firm.

'I'll park myself in the waiting-room.' Martin winked at his brother. 'It's okay, Nurse, I know the way, like the flipping back of me hand!' He went nimbly up the corridor, grinning appreciatively at Nurses Adams and Joiner on the way.

Paul went to sit by the window, turning his back on the Scrabble board. Mr Galleon, in his walking plaster, stomped crossly back to bed. 'I was winning, you know.'

'Never mind, Mr Galleon.' Charis walked along with him. She helped him to bed; this was strictly speaking the ward's quiet time, the time of rest before the visitors came.

Mr Ivyson was reading, lying flat on his back—an awkward angle for seeing print, but he managed it fairly well. His spinal operation had been a success. Good bony fusion had taken place, which meant that during the day he could be lifted from his plaster bed and placed on an ordinary one, with boards beneath the mattress for firm support. He was returned to his plaster every night, but he put up with that. Things weren't too bad, not bad at all . . . one stage at a time, and each of them slow, but never mind, I'll get there in the end, he told himself, turning another page. He laid his book face down on his chest as he saw Staff Nurse Littleton coming across from Ernie Galleon's bed. She was being followed, he noticed, by the surgeon, Mr Morland, and the young houseman who liked to quip and joke. They all three reached his bed at once, and Staff Nurse greeted Mr Morland, asking if he wanted the case notes. Mr Morland shook his head.

'No, I'm not stopping, I'm here to say goodbye to young Dobson, but how are things with you, Mr Ivyson?' He squatted down on a stool.

'All right, sir, no complaints.' William Ivyson took off his glasses. His round, mild, intelligent face had a naked look without them. 'I shall be glad when I'm allowed to sit up,' he rolled his head to the side, 'a view of the ceiling is all very well, but it palls as time goes on.'

'A *long* time too, I appreciate that,' Guy Morland nodded in agreement, 'but as soon as we're sure that your muscle and joint functions are strong enough, we'll have you sitting, then standing, then walking with assistance. How are you getting on with your mobilising exercises?'

'Ah well, that's something else again!' William Ivyson pulled a face, but he agreed, nevertheless, that Mrs Dixon, his physiotherapist, was a good sort, even though she wore him out.

Guy Morland looked worn out himself, Charis thought as they left the bed. He walked as though he would rather be sitting, which was very probably the case. He had been in Theatre since half past eight this morning, Sister had told her that. Quite possibly he had not eaten yet. It was good of him to see Paul. He didn't have to, Rob could have done it; it was fairly unusual for a Registrar to put himself out like this. She wondered if Paul appreciated it. She doubted if he did; he just wanted out, and who could blame him for that?

Rob went off to see the new patients. Paul joined Charis and Guy Morland; he limped towards them, using his elbow crutch.

'Now look, Paul,' said Guy, as they stood outside the office, 'treat that mended knee of yours with a little sensible caution . . . don't go mad. Is that understood?'

'Yes, Mr Morland, sir!' Paul gave a mock salute.

Ignoring his cheekiness, Guy carried on. 'You'll find stopping and starting difficult for a time,' he said, 'just don't try to force the pace. And your physiotherapy appointments are vital. You'll have got your appointments card?'

'Yes, Mr Morland, sir!' Paul recited again. 'Not to worry, I won't put a single foot wrong.'

'It's not your feet I'm worried about,' said Guy with a smile. Charis looked at him curiously; he really minds, she thought, he really cares about the patients, even when they've left. She wished she either liked him more, or didn't admire him so much. Mixed feelings were such uncomfortable things.

They were halfway up the corridor when his bleep began to croak. He turned back to the office, muttering under his breath. 'Hang on for me, Paul,' he called out, 'wait for me at the lifts.'

'Will do,' replied Paul. He and Charis continued steadily on, and were joined by Martin who came out of the waiting-room. The two youths went into a huddle—Martin, it seemed, had a plan. Charis caught snatches of what he was saying—something about swapping places, and a bit of a giggle, and giving His Highness a shock. But what happened next was no fault of hers, she was no part of the trick that they played on Guy Morland, who was in no mood for it. Paul limped into the waiting-room, while Martin stayed where he was, in full view of the corridor and as soon as he saw Guy Morland he began to mark time, to jog on the spot, raising his knees up high, elbows jerking, breath coming out in rasps.

Charis heard her own protesting voice, but most of

it was drowned by a furious command from Guy: '*Paul* stop it, stop it *at once!*'

Martin grinned broadly and stood to attention, while Paul limped out of the waiting-room. Nurses Barford and Adams, who were tidying dressings in Clean Utility, looked out to see what all the noise was about. Rob, not far behind Guy, concealed his laugh with a choke—a spraying splutter that deceived no one, least of all Guy Morland, who turned round on him, telling him to shut up. As for him, he was still suffering from shock, and from anger too, most of the latter directed against himself, for being fooled, even for two seconds flat. 'A good joke, but the wrong time and place,' he remarked quietly. And his glance included Charis, who realised, to her dismay, that he thought she had been part of the silly charade. It was at her he continued to gaze, as he said in deepening tones, 'This is a hospital ward, not a circus ring for clowns.'

'Took you in, though, didn't we?' Paul and Martin spoke as one.

'I admit it,' he laughed then, as he pushed at the corridor doors. 'Come on, I'll see you two comedians out to the lifts. 'But you, Paul,' he wagged a finger, 'are going down in a chair. Fetch one, will you?' He looked at Charis, who went to do his bidding, fully intending, once she got back, to make it very clear that she had *not* been a party to Paul and Martin's prank.

But the opportunity was denied her, for when she returned, dragging a wheelchair from the storage area, it was to find the landing deserted. 'When the lift came up there was a wheelchair in it,' Nurse Barford informed her. 'Paul went down in that, and Mr Morland won't be back. That telephone call was from Accident and Emergency. A motorist has been admitted with a fractured arm and leg. They're preparing him in A and E and Morland's operating.

Sir Rodney's in Harley Street today.'

'I see.' Charis repaired to the office. It just never
stops, she thought. She wondered if Guy would have
any respite before getting back on the job. But of
course there was Sister Tolbie; she mustn't forget
Joanne. She would ply him with coffee and sandwiches, down in Theatre's resting-room. There was no
need, no need at all, for Charis to worry. Sighing a
little she opened the office door.

Rob had left Mr Clover's and Mr Renner's notes
on the desk. She sat down to read them, but had no
sooner started than Dr Blane, the anaesthetist, steered
himself importantly into the room. He was a big man,
with a bow front, and a habit of wearing his glasses,
the rimless kind, halfway down his nose. Realising
why he had come, Charis passed the notes over to
him. He would want all the details, all the findings,
about the two new patients. He alone would be
responsible for their anaesthesia, on Thursday morning
when they went down to Theatre. Details of blood
count, urine analysis, TPR and blood pressure, were
all there. He asked about X-rays. Charis handed them
to him, with reports attached, then took him into the
ward. There he examined both patients, and talked
with them for some time. It was very nearly three
o'clock, and the first of the visitors had begun to
arrive before Dr Blane took himself off. He had no
sooner gone than a timid tap, scarcely more than a
scratch, sounded on the office door. Charis thought
she knew who it was. And yes, sure enough, it was
Mrs Galleon with a box of new-laid eggs for Mr
Galleon: 'For my Ernie, and I've marked them all
with a cross. I don't want them mixed up with anyone
else's . . . you *will* see he gets the right ones?' She
said this every single Thursday, her day for bringing
the eggs, and each time either Sister Holt, or Charis,
solemnly promised, hand on heart, that her wishes
would be carried out.

By now the ward had several visitors. Mr Ivyson's wife had come, so had their daughter Melissa, who was reading law at St Saviour's. She was very clever and they were justly proud of her. Mrs Galleon, who had followed them in, was dusting a chair with her handkerchief. Mr Renner and Mr Clover had two visitors each, one of them a baby girl, quite plainly Mr Clover's; she had his dark brown hair and laughing eyes. Paul's bed had been stripped and washed; it wouldn't be empty for long. Most probably the accident case now in Theatre would be its new occupant some time later tonight.

In spite of all the trouble Paul had caused, Charis knew she would miss him, not to mention his cheeky brother, who had never failed to visit. The two boys had a window-cleaning business, they had built it up from scratch. Sitting there drinking her tea for five minutes, Charis pulled a notepad towards her and did a quick, slashing sketch of the scene that had taken place . . . of Martin doing his 'knees-up' act at the top of the corridor, of Paul peeping out of the waiting-room, of Guy Morland rushing towards them, steam puffs ejected from his mouth. He was very sketchable, with his straight dark looks, the way he stepped out and carried himself, the angle of his jaw. It amazed her how clearly her mind's eye saw him, how easily that image projected itself from brain, to arm, to fingers, to pencil and pad. The result was a cruel caricature, but even so the likeness was there; that spiky, forked lightning outline was unmistakably Guy Morland's, so was the face, led by his thrusting jaw. A touch of mischief and malice made Charis scrawl a caption across the sketch . . . 'SO WHO LOOKED THE BIGGEST FOOL?' It was one *good* way, she thought, of getting him out of her system. Grabbing her tray, she carried it kitchenwards.

Molly Silver, the domestic, was in the kitchen, loading crockery into the washer. It had only recently

been installed, and Molly was wary of it. She switched
it on and stood well back, she even crossed herself, as
though she thought the monster might explode.

The afternoon passed to early evening, when the
newsvendor arrived—a youth Charis knew. She let
him go into the ward. The afternoon visitors had long
since gone, but a few more would trickle in at seven
o'clock, just for half an hour. Meantime, there were
the TPRs and four-hourly treatments to do. Charis
summoned Anne Varden, a second-year nurse, to help
her turn Mr Palfrey, who had a stable vertebral
fracture, which distorted the line of his spine. In order
to minimise pain the greatest care had to be taken
whenever he needed to be moved. The relationship
between spine and pelvis had to be maintained; this
was done by rolling the patient from one side to the
other, avoiding any bending of his back. Donald
Palfrey was a natural stoic, and bore his discomforts
well. The only thing he complained about, *bitterly,*
was the food. He wanted to know what was for
supper, and groaned in mock agony when told it was
salad or macaroni cheese.

Rob was in the office, Charis could see him standing
with his back to the viewing window as she and Nurse
Varden passed. She tapped on the glass, and he turned
and came out, and standing in the corridor he told
her about the new case—the fractured arm and leg
motorist—who would be coming up from the recovery
room as soon as his bed was prepared. 'I rather think
Morland will pay you a visit. He's got what notes
there are. Here he is now—cripes, that was quick! I'd
better have a word.' Rob set off up the corridor and
met Guy halfway. They conversed together, then Rob
went off, while Guy came down to Charis, walking
slowly, and dressed, she noticed, for going home at
last. A light fawn anorak covered the jacket of his
suit. He hadn't bothered to zip it up and it bunched
round his back, giving him a huddled and even more

weary look. They walked into the office together, and he handed her the papers which would start off Mr Peter Trueman's notes. 'You'll need a Balkan frame for his arm, it'll have to be up for two days. His leg's not in traction, just held between sandbags. It's an upper-third femur break, fixed by intramedullary nail.'

'When is he coming up?' asked Charis.

'Any minute . . . better get your minions cracking.'

She did so, then went back to him. He was sitting behind the desk, his face nearly the same putty hue as his anorak. 'I'll get some coffee brought through,' she said firmly, but he told her not to bother. 'The thought is kind, but I'm eating out.' He glanced up at her and smiled. Usually it was she looking up at him, the reversal of positions made a subtle difference, made him appear a little more approachable. That business with Paul and his twin was none of my doing, she wanted to say, but she managed to stem the words. This wasn't the time to bother him—not after the kind of day he had obviously had. He might have forgotten the whole episode, at least for the time being, but if he had, he was soon reminded, for as he got up from the desk he dislodged a piece of paper that had adhered to the back of the folder. It floated down, literally to his feet. He picked it up without much interest, but as he did so he stiffened; so did Charis, for she could see what it was—the paper he held in his hand was the caricature she had done of him and the twins.

'Oh dear!' She gave a silly laugh, and tried to take it from him. His grip on it tightened, then, just as suddenly, he practically thrust it at her.

'Your handiwork, I take it?' he said in brittle tones. He was looking at her, *down* at her now, in every sense of the word; his gaze was scathing, his mouth moved in angry lines.

'It was a fun thing, surely you can see . . . '

'I can see you have a great talent . . . your talent is undeniable! Perhaps you're in the wrong job. Perhaps, to use a time-worn expression, you've missed your true vocation!' As he fastened his anorak the sound of the zip seemed to tear the air between them. Charis itched to do the same with the sketch, which she still held in her hand and couldn't get rid of, like Lady Macbeth's damned spot.

'I did it on the spur of the moment,' she explained.

'Ah, yes, of course! But then so many of your moments appear to be spurred!' he remarked sarcastically, just as the telephone rang.

He lifted the receiver, probably because he was standing nearest to it, or because he wasn't thinking properly. Charis heard him say: 'Yes, she is.' She moved forward, but he practically pushed her back, raising his hand in that staying, annoying way he had. He moved away, wary-faced, the receiver pressed to his cheek. It was bad news, that much was plain, the comments he made were guarded—the first being followed by: 'Yes, I see . . . yes, of course I'll tell her . . . all right, Sister. Yes, I'll bring her down.'

'Is it Mr Trueman? Has he collapsed? Why do they want me?' The receiver went down, and she gasped out the questions, knowing it was fear that sliced into her, cutting the strength from her limbs. She knew the call hadn't concerned a patient . . . she knew it was personal. It concerned *her*. Something had happened . . . something terrible had happened. 'What is it . . . tell me!' she said anxiously.

'Sit down.'

'I don't want . . . ' but Guy pressed her into a chair, the easy chair, the relatives' chair, and he squatted down in front of it. Then, taking her hands and making her look straight into his eyes, he told her the news.

'I'm afraid your father has died.'

'But he can't have! He can't have!' She had to deny

it, she had to say no . . . and no . . . she had to refute it, refuse to accept the truth.

'I'm sorry, my dear,' he drew her up, supporting her as she stood, 'he died an hour ago, at your home. Your sister and brother-in-law had just arrived, they sent for an ambulance, but nothing could be done. It sounds like a massive coronary, and as you and I both know . . .'

'Are they here . . . Nan and Harold?'

'In Sister's office, down in Emergency.'

'I must go!'

'I'll come with you.' He held fast to her arm, then opening the office door he accosted Nurse Barford, who was coming out of the sluice. 'Take over here until the night shift comes on. If you're worried ring the Nursing Officer, explain that Charis has had bad news, she won't be coming back.'

'My father's died, Peggy,' Charis heard herself say, and saying it made it real. So did the sight of Nan's distraught face when they got down to A and E. Harold was there, sitting close to her, while Sister Casualty was hovering, and a tray of tea stood on the desk untouched.

'We did all we could,' Harold told Charis sadly. 'All the first aid things, the kiss of life, and heart massage, before the ambulance came. They said we did all the right things.'

'Sometimes nothing can be done,' Charis assured him, kissing her sister, feeling protective towards her.

'We've sent for Neil,' Nan clung to her hand, 'we thought you'd want him here.' As she spoke the door opened behind Guy's back to admit an ashen-faced Neil. Rain sparkled on his hair, appeared in dark blobs on his jacket. As he stumbled forward over the carpet, as Charis moved towards him, Guy slipped quietly from the room.

CHAPTER FOUR

'I'M so sorry about your father.' Joanne Tolbie stopped
Charis in the transfer bay of Theatre Block, ten days
later. Charis had brought a patient down for his
replacement surgery, which Sir Rodney was
performing, assisted by Robert Peele. This was Charis's first time on duty since that terrible evening when
Guy had told her about her father's death.

Not unnaturally she felt depressed, but glad to be
back at work. The trouble was that just about everyone
said the same thing as Sister Tolbie. Still, they could
hardly ignore the matter, even Charis saw that. 'Guy
said you'd taken it awfully well, but don't push yourself too much.' Joanne, in theatre cap and gown, on
the sterile side of the line, nodded goodbye, and Charis
went back to the ward.

Sister Holt was on duty, and she watched Charis
carefully as she set about her tasks. The girl looked
wan, thin in the face, but she seemed to be in control.
Sister's concern was not without a shade of selfishness.
She was due to go on leave in May, and while she
was away the Littleton girl would be in charge, would
be acting up for her, would be Acting Sister for the
space of two whole weeks.

Charis was popular with the patients, especially the
long-staying ones. Mr Ivyson, now allowed to sit up,
produced a box of chocolates. 'The wife thought you'd
like them,' he said awkwardly, patting Charis's arm.
'We've missed you, we both have, and Melissa asked
after you.'

'Thank you, it's nice to be missed.' Charis's answer

was stiff, but William Ivyson, who was nobody's fool, understood why this was. He wondered what Melissa would do if *he* suddenly died, but the thought was so untenable he thrust it from his mind. Adjusting his headphones, he switched on his radio.

Mr Galleon had been discharged while Charis was away, but even he had left her a present—a hyacinth in a pot. It had grown rather tall and anaemic, but the card attached to it was nicely worded: 'Good luck, and God bless. We're sorry about your loss, with many thanks from Ernest and Elsie G.'

At half past ten Dilys came and dragged her off to coffee. She too said she had missed her. 'It's good to have you back. Did everything go off all right yesterday?' Dilys meant the funeral. She stirred her coffee, watching Charis's face.

'It was horrible, but yes, I suppose . . . yes, it went off all right. We tried to keep it just family, but Father's two partners came, and one or two people he knows in the town . . . *knew* in the town,' Charis amended quickly, taking a gulp from her cup.

'Are you still living at Cranleigh?' asked Dilys.

'Why yes, of course I am. Nan's been with me, so far, going through Father's things, but she'll go back to the Nurseries tomorrow. I can hardly expect her to live apart from Harold, just to keep me company, and I don't want to live with them. That again, I think, is hardly fair. Anyway, Homer will keep me company, and Mrs Kent, our daily, will be there until we've got things sorted out.'

'I expect you'll sell the house when you get married and move over to Kingsford?' Dilys was burning to know how much her friend might have inherited. 'It's a lovely house, it should make a bomb,' she added, thinking Neil Chambers was likely to strike it rich.

'I've not thought as far ahead as that,' Charis said shortly. In actual fact neither Nan nor she knew the contents of their father's will. 'It was something he never mentioned,' Nan had said last week, as she cleared Cedric's desk and assembled the papers for Mr Pratt, the solicitor, who held the will at his office in Princes Parade. 'But he's bound to have left you the house, Charis—it's your home, after all. I've probably been left a chunk of investments, easily encashable. Harold and I can do with some capital to plough into the business. I know it's awful to speculate, but life goes on, you know.' And then she had said almost word for word what Dilys was saying now. 'The house sale will make a nice little nest-egg for you and Neil to start off with.' She said it in Neil's hearing too, which could have been embarrassing. Not that Neil had seemed embarrassed, he had simply enquired when they were having their meeting with Mr Pratt. It was this evening, at five o'clock, and Charis was dreading it. I shall leave all the talking to Nan, she decided, as she got up from the table and followed Dilys out to the landing and lifts.

At lunchtime, feeling unequal to facing the crowd in the dining-room, she bought a sandwich from the hospital shop and made her way to the river. Here she walked along the towpath as far as the wooden seat opposite the Keats Hotel on the farther bank. It was a still day, chilly, but sunny; the sights and sounds of April were all about her—the pellucid sky, the filming of green on the trees, the spawning life in the river itself, the occasional audible plop as a fish surfaced, or a water-rat swam to his hole.

Neil was uppermost in her thoughts, as she sat there on the seat. No one could have been more supportive than he, once he had got over the shock. But the strain had obviously told on him, for during the whole of yesterday he had looked upset to the point of anger; emotions sometimes run close. He was quiet and had not stayed long at the house after the funeral—unlike her father's two partners, Mr Carver and Mr Shaw, who had lingered on, looking suitably glum, making all the right noises, praising their erstwhile partner to the skies. 'But they didn't fool me,' Nan said to Charis afterwards. 'Underneath all that unctuousness they were chortling with glee at the thought of running Hansons on their own.'

On the whole, Charis mused, it was a good thing that Neil would be going to Kingsford—because she had a feeling that he and those two might not see eye to eye. Neil wasn't always the yes-man he seemed, he had a mind of his own. She was pondering on this when a long shadow pooled itself over her feet, and a voice she knew asked if he might sit down.

'Of course, please do.' It was Guy Morland. Her heartbeat settled down—well, almost—and she shouldn't, she realised, have been so surprised to see him. She wasn't far from Mayfield Court, and Rob had told her this morning that G.M. was having today, which was Thursday, off.

He was wearing casual clothes, she noticed, as he lowered himself to the seat. His jeans were light grey, they lay smooth and close along the length of his thigh. His jersey was dark green and chunky, it hugged his throat and ears, thrust his sleek hair up at the back, outlined the cut of his jaw. His profile, against the backcloth of palely burgeoning trees, reminded her of the sketch she had done. She longed to do another—a true one, with no distortions, no mean, cheap little caption. Even now she could still feel shame about that sketch. It was an odd thing about tragedy, it didn't wipe anything out, it obscured other happenings, just for a time, or reduced them in size and importance, but back they swam, as large as life, and every bit as harrowing, as soon as there was time and room for thought.

Scouring her mind for things to say, she remembered to thank him for the note of condolence he had sent to Nan and herself. 'It was kind of you,' she said.

'The least I could do.' The seat planks moved as he

shifted. His hands were clasped between his knees—well kept, strong-fingered hands. One of the ribbed cuffs of his jersey had a loose loop of wool; he had maybe caught it on his watch when he dressed. She fixed her gaze on it, as he spoke again, as he went on to talk about her father. 'I just met him the once,' he told her, 'at the Stantons' housewarming party. We talked about the incredible price of land in the Lincolnshire Fens.'

'It was Father's pet subject. He lived and breathed work.' Charis looked across the river. One or two people were bringing out chairs on to the hotel's patio. She saw them through a mist of tears, which she hastily blinked away. 'He and I were only just beginning to know one another. I was brought up by Nan and Harold, then I went away to train. I had no long stretches of time with Father, not until this year. It was his idea that I should try to get a nursing post at Seftonbridge. I came just before Christmas eighty-four.'

'Fifteen or sixteen months ago.'

'Yes.'

'You'll be glad you did what he asked.'

'I came because of Neil,' she explained. 'He was here working at Hansons. I'd met him before, on short visits. Father introduced us. I . . . liked him. I came home because of Neil.'

'Nevertheless, it pleased your father?'

'Oh yes—yes, it did.'

'Then if I were you I'd stop having a conscience about motives. Stop querying reasons. You did what he asked. Why not be glad about that?' There was an edge to Guy's voice that stopped the gathering ache in Charis's throat. It also stopped foolish confidences. What a harsh man he was! He *could* be kind, but only professionally. He measured his kindness out, drop by drop, with exceeding care. It was all part and parcel of the bedside manner he'd taken years to acquire.

'I must go,' she said, springing up from the seat.

'I'll walk with you as far as the bridge.' He towered above her, making her feel midget-sized again.

'There's no need.' She was making great play of brushing down her coat.

'I'm going that way, as it happens. Don't be tiresome, Charis.' And now he was humouring her, talking to her as though she was six years old. 'Come on, quick march!' He turned her round, then gripping her elbow, he set off beside her, matching his step to hers. In a flash she remembered another occasion when he had seized her by the arm and marched her along, over a carpet, in a certain department store. She wondered if he had ever managed to match his blue necklace. And why had he wanted to, anyway? How very, very odd that she had never stopped to ask herself that before. Ask *him!* Never, never, she thought, never in a million years. She missed a step, and half-stumbled. 'Steady!' she heard him say. 'You don't want a dip in the river at this time of year!' He moved her round to his other side, with such swiftness that she gasped. He appropriated her shoulder bag too . . . he really *had* got a nerve! Masterful Morland, that's what she'd call him, when she did another sketch.

He began to ask her about Margaret Brodie. 'Is she still away?' he enquired. 'There are no lights in her flat in the evenings, and without in any way spying, one can't help noticing these things. I knew she was on a long holiday, she told me that herself, but I thought she might have come home when she knew about your father.'

'The thing is,' Charis said quickly, 'the thing is, she *doesn't* know. We've been very worried, Neil and I, because we can't get in touch. We thought she was spending the whole five weeks with her parents in Aberdeen, but when we rang, her mother told Neil she'd only been with them three days. After that she'd

gone off with friends on a touring holiday in France,
leaving no addresses. It seems that was the idea . . .
to be perfectly free, and out of touch. Her mother was
quite upset. It'll be another three weeks from now
before she'll be back at her flat.'

'Bad news keeps.' Guy's comment was short, but
Charis latched on to it.

'That's exactly what I said,' she agreed, 'that was
my feeling exactly. I realise that Margaret will be
upset and shocked that she didn't know at once, but
if she'd known it would have ruined her holiday, she'd
have come hurrying back, and what for? She couldn't
have helped, she couldn't have done anything. She
needs her break, she really does, she was very over-
worked!' Taken advantage of, in fact, she thought to
herself. Men didn't always think, or care, basically
they were selfish. Why, even Neil had been outraged
when he was told that Margaret Brodie was footloose
and fancy-free in France. He hadn't been best pleased,
either, at Harold's spot-on comment of: 'Well, I'm
damned, the worm has turned at last!'

Charis and Guy, still in a state of precarious agreement, parted company at the bridge. Charis, as she
set off down Silver Street, found herself recalling every
shade and nuance of their conversation from the time
Guy had sat on the seat to just now when he had
flipped a goodbye and walked off through the trees.
He was disturbing—dangerously so, and not just
because of his looks. There was something very much
more to him than the cut of jib and jaw. He had a
power-driven personality, in itself a kind of allure. He
breathed it out through every pore—quite possibly,
she thought, knowing its effect, and glorying in it. Oh,
put him out of your mind! She crossed Princes Parade
in a darting rush, and was sworn at by the driver of a
laundry van, who nearly ran her down.

Romance was blossoming in the ward, so she learned
at visiting-time. 'Between Melissa Ivyson and Mr

Trueman,' Peggy Barford told her. 'Peter Trueman is a solicitor, he's with Mathieson & Pratt.'

'Yes, I know that, and Neil knows him through working next door to him. He looks very young to have qualified.'

'You've not looked at his date of birth. He's twenty-six and Lissa, as they call her, is nearly twenty. She's studying law at St Saviour's. That obviously gives them something in common.'

Including starry eyes, thought Charis, glancing in their direction as she sat at the ward desk. Melissa had abandoned her father, and was sitting by Mr Trueman's bed. They weren't holding hands, weren't touching, but their wish to do just that was so apparent it was laughable, or tear-jerking, perhaps, depending on how one viewed such things, or what memories they invoked. Charis could remember her first romance, remember the magic and thrill—the highs and lows, the meetings and partings, the cloud nine euphoria, the impossible pitch and intensity of it all. I wouldn't change places with Melissa Ivyson for all the gold in Fort Knox, she thought. Charis's dive into introspection was halted by the arrival of the theatre porters wheeling Mr Boston, the hip replacement patient, slowly and carefully into the ward. He had been placed in his bed down in Theatre, his legs separated by a Charnley wedge pillow to reduce the possible risk of dislocation. A blood transfusion had been started, he was conscious, but very drowsy; he was also confused, which was very common after deep anaesthesia. 'You're just fine, Mr Boston,' Charis reassured him, 'you've nothing to worry about. You're back in the ward with all your friends, you're going to be all right.' Seeing the radiance of her smile less than a foot from his face, Simon Boston wondered if, after all, he was in the company of angels. Smiling back, he drifted off to sleep.

'Talk about exhausting!' sighed Rob back in the

office. He had been in theatre for close on six hours,
assisting Sir Rodney Barks. He had watched him
replace the upper end of Mr Boston's thighbone with
a false head, fixed on with acrylic cement. The socket
had been similarly replaced, making a new false joint,
which would work with ease and give no discomfort,
once healing had taken place. 'By the time you and I
are old, Charis, there won't be a single thing, not a
single organ that can't be replaced . . . now that's a
thought, isn't it? I suppose that means we'll never die,
unless we're squashed flat in an accident.'

'Oh, shut up, Rob!' Charis shuddered as she thought
of the laundry van. She fetched Rob some tea with
her eye on the clock. It wouldn't be very long now
before she and Nan were making their way to Nigel
Pratt's office. She felt sick and tried to concentrate
solely on Rob.

'Of course Morland could have done as good a job
as Sir Rodney,' he went on. 'He and Tolbie are a
great team, work together like the same hand and
brain. She's a very good Theatre Sister, you know,
and she keeps her staff on their toes. I'm not surprised
G.M. has got the hots for her. One thing leads to
another, and out of her swaddling robes she's quite a
dish, I wouldn't mind her myself!'

'She's very attractive,' Charis agreed, repeating the
words she had said to Neil five weeks ago on the night
of the Stantons' party. Leaving Rob to slurp his tea
and crack on a ginger biscuit, she went into the ward
to take another look at Mr Boston, and to ask Nurse
Joiner to sit with him for a while. Ten minutes later
she signed off duty, had a last word with Peggy
Barford, then changing into a skirt and jacket, and
short cuffed boots, she left the ward and took the lift
downstairs.

Nan, in a black and white tweed coat, with a velvet
collar and beret, was waiting by the revolving doors,
a briefcase under her arm. The two of them set off

down Princes Parade in the late afternoon sunshine, Nan chatting nervously and ceaselessly. Charis had calmed down. Apart from a thrust of misery at the sight of her father's car being driven out of Hanson's yard by Mr Julius Carver, she had the feeling of being untouchable. The Rover belonged to Hansons', so Mr Carver had every right to use it. Even so, he had claimed it very speedily, collecting it from Cranleigh only three days after her father had died.

Mr Nigel Pratt's office was modern, all tubular chrome and leather, with the sort of chairs that made his clients appear to be sitting on air, with nothing under their rears to keep them up. He was seventy, white-haired, dark-suited, big-nosed and kindly. He had known the Littleton family for many years. The will that lay on his blotter had been drawn up by himself, just over twenty-four years ago when Charis had been born. Twice since then Mr Pratt had suggested, with suitably tactful diffidence, that his client might like to update his will, reconsider it, perhaps. On both occasions the reply he had got had been only just less than offensive. 'If and when I want to change it, Nigel, you'll get the job, never fear.' Mr Pratt could hear Cedric saying the words, see his tight little mouth opening and shutting beneath his clipped moustache.

Charis and Nan, sipping tea, which neither of them wanted, mentally urged Mr Pratt to begin, to get on with the job in hand. In a bid to get him started Nan place the bulging briefcase containing certain of their father's papers on the corner of the desk. 'I'm sure you'll find everything you want there. Everything was in order.' Her voice cracked a little. She was feeling the strain; Charis could see her hands, gripped together, showing the knucklebones.

'Your father's will is a simple one,' Mr Pratt began quietly. He reached for a thick vellum foolscap sheet, deckle-edged and folded in three. He straightened it out, and put his glasses on. 'I've had a copy made for each of you,' he passed these over the desk, 'but briefly, and in layman's language, the content of it is that you, Nancy, inherit the house—Cranleigh House and contents. You, Charis, get the sum of ten thousand pounds in cash; while the rest of the estate, the residue, goes to ten different charities in equal proportions, as listed in the will.

As he stopped speaking it seemed to Charis that everything else stopped too. Everything seemed to die in the silence, then Nan's voice cut across it. 'Mr Pratt, my father was a wealthy man. I simply cannot believe that he meant . . . that he intended to leave all that to charity. The house to me, ten thousand to my sister—well, don't you see what that means? It means that about nine-tenths of his assets—at *least* nine-tenths—will go sailing off to . . . off to good causes! I just don't believe he meant that to happen! I don't believe he meant it!' She jerked in her chair and the copy will fell to the floor.

'I understand how you feel, of course.' Mr Pratt's voice, in contrast to Nan's, was low and controlled and very professional—bedside manner again, Charis thought out of a curious flatness that she knew was a form of shock. 'Cranleigh House and contents,' Mr Pratt carried on, 'is a very handsome bequest, you know, with prices as they are now.'

'I know that,' Nan moved back on her chair, bright red patches standing out on her high-cheeked face, as she turned to look at Charis, 'but what about Charis, for goodness' sake. Ten thousand pounds in cash . . . ten thousand pounds! It's unbelievable! Dad simply can't have intended to make such a vast difference between us!' She coughed and nearly choked.

'At the time the will was made,' Mr Pratt interjected smoothly, 'the two bequests would, curiously enough, have been almost equally matched. Since 1962, however, house prices have soared, whereas the pound has reduced in value.'

'I'm pleased with my ten thousand.' Charis found her voice at last. 'We're *surprised* at the will, and yes, of course we're disappointed too.' She added this out of loyalty to Nan, yet felt she betrayed her father. 'But if that's the way Father wanted to leave things, then that's okay by us,' she finished, not daring to look at Nan.

'He must have intended to make a new will.' Nan was calming down with a great effort. What a child Charis was! She wished she would hold her tongue.

'I don't think so, Nancy.' Mr Pratt put the will back into its envelope. 'I touched on the matter with your father as short a time ago as last summer, but no, he didn't want to alter things. He said if he did, he would let me know. I could hardly bring pressure to bear.'

'Then that's the end of it, isn't it?' Charis jumped in again. She made movements to leave, she wanted to leave, she didn't want Nan to argue, or say any more, it was so undignified. The matter was out of their hands anyway. As executor and solicitor, Mr Pratt would proceed according to the will. 'We shall get over it in time,' she smiled, and Nigel Pratt was disarmed. She was like her mother, that vital twenty-year-old girl who had melted even Cedric's stony heart.

'I feel as though I've been punched in the gut,' Nan said as they crossed the road. 'All that money going to charity! Honestly, Charis, it hurts!'

'It was what Father wanted,' Charis said woodenly. 'It's awful, Nan, I know, but when you consider it, he was entitled to do what he liked. It was his money, he made it himself. You've always told me that . . . how he started from nothing and worked his way to the top.'

'Well, yes, but . . . '

'And he always supported those charities that he listed. I admired him for it. I admired him anyway . . . I enjoyed being with him, Nan.'

They crossed the bridge, reached College Walk, and turned left into Challoners Lane. 'I might not mind so much,' said Nan, 'if he'd mentioned it . . . *told* us about it.'

'Yes, you would, and so would I, which is probably why he didn't.'

'So you *do* mind?' Nan gave her chick-and-child sister a motherly glance.

'Of course I do.' For the second time that day Charis blinked against tears. She felt Nan's arm slide through hers, but she couldn't explain how she felt. Everything and everyone seemed to have changed during the last ten days. Even she was different, she felt different, she seemed to see things differently, as though she were using another pair of eyes. She was worried about Neil, terribly worried, worried about telling him that Cranleigh wouldn't belong to her after all. 'I'm living in your house, aren't I?' she realised as they walked up the drive.

'Oh, for God's sake!' Halfway to the garage, Nan turned and hugged her hard. 'It's *your* home for as long as you like—till you and Neil get married. It looks as though he's here already.' She glanced at Neil's blue Datsun on the far side of the circular gravel sweep.

'I wasn't expecting him round tonight,' said Charis.

'Well, don't sound so dismayed!'

'I'm not, it's just that he told me he was going to Norwich to see his parents.'

Nan lifted the up-and-over door, feeling for her keys. She was going home to cook Harold's supper, and tell him what had happened. She couldn't get there fast enough. 'I'll be back about ten,' she said. 'Go in and see Neil, we both of us need our menfolk tonight.' As she backed the car out, Charis went into the house.

Mrs Kent, who seldom went home until six, had shown Neil into the sitting-room. He was standing by the french doors, looking out. He smiled at Charis as she went in; he seemed to be back to normal, which was something—which was everything! 'I was worried about you yesterday,' she told him, as they kissed and sat down on the settee.

'It was a terrible day all round, wasn't it?' He watched her peel off her jacket and drop it on the carpet by Homer, who laid his head on it. Charis wasn't the tidiest of mortals, he had noticed this before. 'The thing was, I had bad news,' he explained, picking up the coat, 'and I let it override everything else, which of course I shouldn't have. I'm sorry, darling . . . I really am.' As he laced his fingers in hers he felt the rubbing roughness of the diamond engagement ring he had bought for her just over six months ago.

'What kind of bad news?' she alerted at once, 'not *your* family too?'

'No, no, nothing like that—oh no, my people are fine.' He turned his head and looked at her; he had marvellously clear blue eyes, they were magnified by his glasses, which also seemed to guard them, or make them look guarded; Charis found herself holding her breath. What now, she thought . . . what now . . . what now? And then she heard him say: 'I'm not going to get the partnership . . . they told me yesterday.'

'Neil!' She stared at him, thunderstruck. Anger flushed his cheeks.

'No partnership, and no branch at Kingsford, by order of Carver and Shaw.'

'But Neil, it was promised! They can't do that!'

'I'm afraid they very well can. It was promised by your father, there was nothing actually signed. The

new office was his idea. It has come to light that
neither of the other two partners ever wanted it. They
went along with it, apparently, when your father
mooted it. Now they can do as they please, and it
doesn't please them to go ahead . . . nor to make
me a partner, although they put it tactfully, said it
was a policy change, and nothing more.'

'But I simply don't understand,' cried Charis. 'Surely
with Father gone, they'll need another partner, surely
they'll need to have three . . . to manage the work,
and everything?' She saw Neil shake his head.

'There will be two partners, and two only—their
goodselves,' he said, not without a sneer in his voice,
and who could blame him for that? 'They've offered
me a raise in salary, but that's just a sop, I think. I
don't want to stay there, not in the long term, it
wouldn't suit me for long. Yesterday I could have
walked out very easily, but I'm not given to grandiose
gestures, and one has to be sensible.'

'Yes, of course, I understand.' Charis squeezed his
hands very tightly. How on *earth* was she going to tell
him about the will?

'The thing is,' he went on, 'it's been such a shock,
on top of everything else.'

He looked bleak, she thought, and far away; she
longed to do something to help. 'I'm just so sorry, it
seems so unfair!' She tried to say the right things. It
was awful for him, so demeaning, he had suffered a
loss of face. No one liked being turned down . . . it
was horrid not to be wanted. He had been looking
forward for such a long time to being part of Hansons,
with a say in its running, which he certainly wouldn't
have now. 'I'm sure they'll regret their decision,' she
said, 'they've made a big mistake.'

'I was awake for the greater part of the night, trying
to think things through.' His throat felt sore, he
cleared it. 'In the end I came up with a plan that
might just work out, Charis . . . work out for us

both, and be far better than Hansons . . . if you agree, of course.'

'What kind of plan?' Suppose, she thought, it was something she *couldn't* agree to? Suppose he wanted to emigrate, start afresh in a new land? How would she feel? What would she say? What would she do? 'What kind of plan?' she repeated.

'I'll tell you later,' he said, 'but tell me now how you and Nan got on at Pratt's. There were no snags there, I hope?'

'It wasn't as we thought. In a way, Neil, it was rather a shock.' She told him what had happened. How would he take it? What would he say? She was very soon to find out. She watched his face lengthen, saw his jaw go slack.

'But that's monstrous . . . *monstrous!*' His voice rose. 'You can't have got it right!'

'Here's the copy will, see for yourself.' She drew the photostat document out of her bag and passed it to him. He read it, frozen-faced.

'You'll contest it, of course . . . you'll change it?' He stabbed the top of the sheet. 'Look at the date . . . look when it was made . . . twenty-four years ago!'

'That doesn't make it challengeable!'

'It does, if it's unfair!'

'No, Neil.'

'Now, listen, Charis . . . you don't understand these things. Your father can't have meant so much to go to charity. He must have meant to review the will, to leave you the house and contents . . . the house and contents, at the very least, and even that on its own would hardly be an over-the-top bequest. Are you sure there's no later will? Have you had a proper look round, searched his things, here and at Hansons? Well, yes, I suppose you have,' he amended quickly, seeing the flash in her eye. 'But I think you should go back and see Pratt, tell him you want to appeal,' he added more quietly, making himself calm down.

Charis's voice was quiet too. 'It was Father's last will,' she said, 'and that being so, we accept it, abide by what it says. If he'd wanted to make a new one, he would have taken the steps to do so. He never overlooked anything, and he never put anything off. So the will must have been his dying wish, he must have had good reason for leaving it exactly as it is. And there's something else too, Neil, that you don't seem to realise. I loved and admired my father. It's *him* I want, not his money. I happen . . . I happen to miss him, very much.' There was silence in the room.

'I miss him too.' Neil's voice came first, sounding flat and subdued. 'It's just that it's very disappointing . . . it's just that I don't like seeing . . . don't like your not getting what you deserve.'

'To tell you the truth, I couldn't care less.' Charis felt deathly tired, suddenly weary, as though a blanket, heavy and smothering, had dropped about her, weighing her into the ground. She made herself move, and switched on the fire. Neil got up as well.

'I shall have to be going, I've got to leave you. It sounds callous, I know, but I'm going to see my people, and if I'm to get to Norwich tonight . . . '

'Of course you must go.' She accepted his kiss, and his face felt icy cold. Perhaps hers did too. She saw him off, aware of a surge of relief. It astonished her that she was actually glad to be left on her own for a while. She needed to think, and she needed to eat. She recalled her meagre lunch.

If she didn't eat she'd be ill, she reasoned, and that would help no one at all. If she was ill she wouldn't be able to work. Her work was all-enduring, always there, and it wouldn't let her down.

Mrs Kent had left a casserole simmering in the oven. So Charis ate in the kitchen in front of the Aga, feeding morsels to Homer, then took her coffee through to the living-room.

It was then she remembered that Neil hadn't explained about his plan—the one he had said would suit them both. She wondered what it was. It had been forgotten by both of them after their argument. It wasn't until much later, long after Nan had come back, that she wondered if Neil's embryo plan needed money for its development—a great deal of money like, for instance, a very substantial nest-egg. And the thought was shaming, she felt ashamed for letting it enter her mind. But it stayed there, though, for most of the night, it persisted even through sleep. It was still there in the morning, clear, and bright, and sharp . . .

It was still there when she reached the Hospital.

CHAPTER FIVE

A FAINT smell of breakfast porridge, bread and butter, and tea still hung about the beds, as Sister, accompanied by Charis, wheeled the drugs trolley into the ward. A chill wind was blowing outside, and Donald Palfrey grumbled as Charis, obeying Sister's instructions, opened one of the windows. 'I'd sooner have a fug than flaming pneumonia!' He gulped his tablets down. Mr Palfrey's back condition was improving with every day that passed. He had physiotherapy, extension exercises, every afternoon. Once his posture had returned to normal, he would be able to be discharged. He still loathed hospital food, and he still loved to grumble.

'Fugs breed germs, Mr Palfrey,' Sister called from the trolley. 'We'll close up again in a minute or two,' her eye ran down the prescriptions: 'Trueman Peter: Ferro.Calmic 100 mgm.' Putting the tablet in a cap container, she handed it to Charis, who also checked it with the list, then took it to Mr Trueman, pouring out some water from his jug.

With the necessary checking, and inevitable chatting, there was no means of hurrying medicines. Nevertheless, Sister chafed with impatience as Charis was delayed, time and again, by patients who wanted a word. It was true she dealt with them speedily, but the clock was racing on. At ten-thirty Sir Rodney Barks, his Registrar and houseman, with heaven knows how many medical students, would be trailing into the ward for the teaching round which took place every week. With this in mind, Charis stopped Nurse Varden, who was frantically tidying beds, and asked her to make quite sure that Mr Trueman's blood report had come up from the labs and was filed away in his notes.

'And if it hasn't, Nurse, get them to give you the details over the phone.' This was Sister again, at least four yards away, peering at her labels. For a tiny lady, her ears were remarkably long.

Sir Rodney and entourage stood around for some minutes, half in and half out of the office, discussing the research that he, Sir Rodney, was currently working on. There was much talk of knees, and rotations, and patellas, of medial pivotal shifts, and quadriceps exercises, not to mention knee locks and osteochondritis dissecans.

Charis knew they were there, she could see them, but she couldn't get out of the ward. They effectively blocked the doorway; there must be six students at least. The medicine round had been finished a good ten minutes ago, but she was talking to Mr Boston, the hip replacement patient, who had had his operation the day before. His blood transfusion had been replaced by a saline drip. He complained of soreness in his arm, and she was inspecting the needle site, when the round started and they all came into the ward. They came in in strict formation—Sister and Sir Rodney in front, Guy Morland a step behind, Rob a step behind him, the medical students in couples—five young men and a girl, who was Chinese, and as pretty as a doll.

They came straight to Mr Boston's bed. Charis made to move away, but Sir Rodney stopped her, by saying how sorry he was about her father. 'A great man, brilliant man . . . sad loss, m'dear.' Then without waiting for thanks or comment, he addressed himself to the patient. 'How are you feeling? Still rough, I expect. It'll pass soon enough . . . get you off this thing tonight,' he pointed to the drip. 'Better for you then—be able to move. We'll fix you up with a pole . . . yes, that's right, like that chap's over there . . . be able to help yourself then. Save wear and tear on the nurses' backs!'

As Charis made her way to Clean Utility, to check the stock of dressings, she couldn't help wondering if Sir Rodney's bark did the patients good or not. Certainly it chivvied them up, jollied them along, she supposed. It also effectively stopped them asking awkward questions or making any tiresome complaints. His approach was different from his Registrar's; Guy Morland lost no time, but he never talked *at* his patients, nor sidestepped their questions, and his voice was the kind that was good to listen to.

She began counting sterile dressings packs, with her mind half on Guy, who had been wearing his impassive face when she passed him in the ward. He was still in her thoughts some ten minutes later when his face, a shade less impassive, appeared round Clean Utility's door. Charis climbed down from the steps with a pile of boxes. She felt she had conjured him up, like Aladdin with his magic lamp . . . not that he looked like a genie; he looked every inch exactly what he was.

'Can we have a word in the office, Staff?'

'Why, yes.' She followed him out.

'They can do without me in there, for a minute,' he nodded towards the ward. 'Sister has just informed me,' he said, closing the office door, 'that you're in charge tomorrow, Saturday.'

'Yes, it's her weekend off. We take it in turns.'

'So I'm sure she'll have told you about the new admission—the disc lesion, Mr Fellowes?'

'She has, and his notes are here, they've just come up from Records. I see from the threatre list that he's down for Tuesday, for laminectomy.'

'Quite right, and what I would like . . . ' He broke off, looking annoyed, as a brief knock on the door was followed by a pink-faced Nurse Adams, who informed Charis that Mr Chambers was on the public phone. 'I told him you were engaged, Staff, but he said it was very important. It's a long-distance call, he's speaking from Norwich.'

'Tell him I'll ring him back.'

'Better answer it, don't you think?' Guy said quietly.

Charis went to do so, furious with Nurse Adams, and hot with embarrassment. But as well as that, she felt alarmed. Neil never rang her at work. Surely nothing else had gone wrong? Her head began to pound, and her hand was slippery as she picked up the telephone.

'Neil, it's Charis . . . whatever's wrong?'

His voice at the Norwich end sounded hoarse and raspy, he was feeling rotten, he had woken up with a cold. 'I shan't be coming back today. I know we were meeting this evening, but can we make it Sunday? I shall stay up here until then.'

'I'm on duty on Sunday, up until four. Neil, I'm sorry about the cold, but I'll have to ring off. I was with someone . . . I can't stop now.'

'I'll come round on Sunday evening,' he croaked.

'Okay, okay, see you then. Take care of yourself,' she remembered to add, before she replaced the phone and went back down the corridor, words of apology on her lips. She was never to give them voice, however, for the office was empty—smack-in-the-face empty, the curtain at the window blowing inwards over the desk, as though to make quite sure she saw the message left there, scribbled on an envelope: 'On second thoughts, Peele can fill you in about John Fellowes.' The initials 'G.M.' were printed at the end.

He couldn't have waited a single minute, he must have written this as soon as I set foot out of the room, Charis thought. He couldn't have waited at all! Looking through the viewing window, she could see him in the ward. He had parted company from Sir Rodney, and with three medics grouped around him, was holding forth at Donald Palfrey's bed.

So that was that. She sat down at the desk, then went in search of Jane Adams. 'Never do that again, Nurse,' she told her. 'Never, ever come into the office and interrupt when I'm talking to someone else!'

'I just thought, Staff—' The girl looked upset.

'Just never do it again!' Charis repeated, and Jane went off to find her friend Anne Joiner, and tell her what a foul mood Staff was in.

The teaching round took over an hour, and by the time it was done, by the time the surgeons and embryo surgeons had gone their separate ways, the big heated luncheon trolleys had come down from the kitchens, and Charis was back in the ward supervising meals.

Later, up in the nurses' dining-room—for she could hardly avoid it for ever—she ran the gamut of more expressions of sympathy from colleagues. 'Do you think you'll get married sooner, now, before you move to Kingsford?' asked Dilys, tucking into her pie.

'As a matter of fact, Dilys,' Charis said carefully, 'the Kingsford project is off. There've been policy changes at Hansons; there's not to be a new branch.'

'Does that mean you'll be staying here?' As Dilys saw Charis nod, she dropped her fork on her plate with a clatter. 'But, Charis, that's terrific, it's super, really *super!* I just couldn't be more pleased! So when will you be getting married, then?'

'We've not settled a date yet. We'll most likely talk about it on Sunday evening, when Neil comes round to the house.' She hoped Dilys wouldn't probe any more, but touched by her reaction to the news that she wouldn't be moving, she decided to explain that Cranleigh and contents had been left to her sister, but that she herself had a legacy, a cash one that would be very useful indeed.

'Oh, I'd rather have hard cash any day. I should think a cash legacy's better,' spluttered Dilys, clearly envisaging an exceedingly handsome sum, and envying

Charis who, in spite of it all, had a face as white as a sheet. 'You ought to have had another week off, love.' She looked at her anxiously. 'Are you on duty this weekend?'

'Yes, until Sunday at four. I'm seeing Neil then.'

'You said that before.'

'I'm woolgathering,' Charis smiled uneasily. She wondered what Dilys would say if she told her that in all probability Neil and she would never get married, just stay engaged for years. Without her father to buttress him, without his continued support, without the promise of a partnership, or herself inheriting wealth, Neil might never dare to set a date.

We aren't in love, she thought sadly, we're friends and we get along well, but we aren't *in* love, and we never have been. Is affection enough to marry on? If Neil came back from Norwich and said, 'Let's get married next month,' what would she say, what would she do, how would she react? Questions like these, questions that perhaps she should have asked before, sat in her mind for the next two days, pushing out sleep at night, sending her off to work with heavy eyes and a leaden heart. Once on the ward a kind of ease came, for her thoughts transferred themselves to other people's problems, to other people's pain . . . physical pain that she could help to relieve.

But when Sunday afternoon came round, as she bicycled home in the rain—a thick mizzle of rain that an English April often brings—she knew that whatever Neil said, she couldn't marry him. She knew she had got to break the engagement; she just prayed she would find the right words—words that would make him feel reprieved and not too let down, words that wouldn't hurt his pride, at least not for very long. He had been let down badly over the partnership, so ought she to delay? Ought she to wait a little bit longer? Yes, even now she was trying to find an excuse for not doing what she must. I have to do it, I just have to do it, she thought. He may not mind at all. Thus did she try to bolster her courage as she changed out of her uniform into a light wool dress, and went downstairs.

She looked at her watch. Neil was late. She busied herself feeding Homer, who always had his meal at five o'clock. How silent the house was, how empty it felt. Only Homer's gluttonous champing, as he ate his lamb and biscuits, broke the hush. Giving him a bowl of fresh water, Charis went through to the sitting-room, just in time to see Neil's car turning into the drive.

I shan't be able to do it . . . I can't . . . I shan't be able to do it! She panicked, as she watched him getting out—big and tall and blond, hunching his shoulders against the falling rain.

They greeted one another, Neil keeping his distance. 'You don't want to catch my cold,' he told her. Charis made tea, and they sat down and drank it, he doing most of the talking, telling her about his mother who had taken on more pupils; she was a music teacher, a gifted pianist. 'She and Dad sent their love,' he finished, leaning forward in his chair to set his empty tea cup on the tray.

Tell him now, she thought. Tell him now . . . *begin,* get it over with. Her mouth felt so dry that her lips stuck together, even her tongue felt welded, tight and useless against the roof of her mouth. 'Neil,' she managed to get out at last, but he spoke at the self-same moment, and went on speaking, staring down at the rug.

'I've been doing some serious thinking over the weekend,' he said. 'Well, I've more or less *had* to, not getting the partnership, and with everything being so changed. It takes time to recover from that sort of thing, time to reorientate. I know we said we'd get married this summer, but in view of all that's happened, I think we ought to put things off, not fix on anything definite. I don't suppose you want to rush things, do you?' His eyes met hers anxiously.

'I don't think we ought to marry at all, Neil. I think we should call it off.' In the end her words came out flatly and baldly, for what he had just said made things more easy, made her part more simple, or more inevitable. She went on to explain, noting the flit of expressions across his face. Surprise came first, then indignation, followed by relief. In different, less poignant circumstances, Charis might have laughed. 'You agree with me, don't you?' she prompted at the end.

'It's the last thing I expected!' Neil stared at her, red-faced, but she felt his agreement was tacit in his reply.

'We made a mistake,' she added gently, 'but we've found it out in time. You do see that, don't you, Neil?'

He shook his head, mystified. 'It seems sad to me that all we've had, all we've done together, can be lumped together and called a mistake!' He snatched off his glasses, staring down at her shoulder-bag on the floor.

'The mistake was in deciding to marry, deciding to get engaged. We were never in love, we were good friends—*are* good friends,' she corrected. 'There's love between us of a . . . a kind, but it's simply not strong enough.'

'That's a little too deep for me, I'm afraid,' he was looking indignant again, 'but yes, of course, as you feel as you do, of course we must break the engagement.'

Charis rummaged in her bag; her ring was in it. She produced it, and held it out. 'Thank you,' he said, and took it. It was all very businesslike. In a minute we'll be shaking hands, she thought, following him to the door. 'Don't come out in the rain, it's not worth it,' said Neil on the front door steps. He ran down them, turning up his collar, and slammed himself into the car. She waited until he had driven away, then went back into the sitting-room. She wondered what she had worried about, why she had fretted so much. It had all gone off so smoothly and easily. Breaking engagements, she thought, is a piece of cake . . .

And then she burst into tears.

'But you and Neil are so well matched,' Nan said worriedly. It was the following Tuesday, and she and Charis were lunching at the Crown, a short distance away from the Hospital. Nan was in Seftonbridge shopping, a rare occurrence for her, but Harold needed one or two things which she couldn't get at Molding, and she had bought some stout brogue shoes for herself. 'When you rang and told me you'd decided to split up, I simply couldn't believe it.' She was very concerned about Charis, she wanted to see her settled, especially now, with their father gone, and Cranleigh to be sold—as it would be, as soon as probate was through.

'It wasn't a sudden decision, Nan,' Charis told her calmly. 'I miss Neil, of course I do. I miss being engaged, but things just didn't work out, that's all.' She didn't say any more. She had never told Nan about Neil's outburst over the will, which had pushed her to make the move she had.

'I wasn't in love with Harold when we married,' Nan said suddenly, 'I married him out of pique, and annoyance—more than that . . . fury, I think, because Dad married so soon after Mother was killed.'

Charis stared at her. 'I never knew that!'

'Oh, things turned out all right. I fell in love with him, fathoms deep, after the first three weeks, and stayed that way,' Nan smiled as her foot touched the parcels under the table. Even now, after twenty-five years, a quarter of a century, Nan still got pleasure from buying Harold's vests.

'Why have you never told me before? Didn't you like my mother?' For the first time since she had broken with Neil, Charis's thoughts were off him, divorced from him, as they focused themselves on Nan. 'Didn't you like my mother?' she repeated, laying down her fork.

'I grew to like her. We became friends, we were the same age, bar three weeks. She was far too young for Father; he worshipped her, I might add, as I did you from the first moment I held you in my arms. Bringing you up completed our happiness. So what I want to know,' Nan went on, wiping her embarrassed-hot face, 'is exactly what you're planning to do now.'

'Carry on with my life, carry on with my job, and eventually buy a small flat. I shall put my legacy, when I get it, down as a deposit, and apply for a mortgage. I'm sure I shall get one. I want my very own place. I decided on this yesterday.' Charis looked anxiously at her sister. She wanted her blessing, and no more talk about Neil.

'A flat?' Nan's eyes met hers. 'Well, yes, I suppose that makes sense. You can do worse than put your money into property, as I'm sure . . . oh, never mind.' She bit back the words she was going to say. 'As I'm sure Neil would tell you', had been on the tip of her tongue; she was going to have to guard it well. 'And when you get your flat you can have what you like from Cranleigh,' she said, 'furniture, fittings, carpets, rugs, anything you choose. At least I can do *that* for you, and sucks to Mr Pratt!'

'Mr Pratt won't know!' They giggled together.

'Let's make a deal,' said Nan. 'You stay at Cranleigh and keep out squatters, till the will's proved, and I can sell. I'll keep Mrs Kent on, pay her wages, and when you move out, I'll ask her if she'd like to work for Harold and me at the Nurseries. She's got her own car, she might agree.'

'Yes, I think she might,' agreed Charis.

'So how does that suit you? What do you say?'

'Done!' Charis said solemnly, and they shook hands over the coffee cups.

They parted company at the Hospital gates, and Nan walked on, her russet head stuffed with thoughts of Charis getting back with Neil. She had little of her sister's discernment, she lacked imagination; solid and dependable, she judged everyone by herself. Of course they would get together again. Charis had been upset . . . the past two weeks had been a nightmare time for them all, and no one would understand that better than Neil. Whether Charis bought a flat or not—and it might take time to find one—Nan was quite sure, completely convinced, that once the dust had settled Neil would woo and win Charis all over again.

John Fellowes, the disc lesion patient, had come up from Theatres, and was being wheeled into the ward, as Charis got out of the lift. She wondered if Guy Morland had finished his list for the day. She supposed so, as she knew he had an outpatients' clinic at two. She had seen him yesterday when he came to the ward to see Sir Rodney's patient, Mr Boston, the hip replacement, who had developed perineal swelling, for which Guy recommended a scrotal support. Charis had escorted him into the ward, making a note of all he said. Their conversation had been 'patients only', which suited her perfectly. If he had unbent even the slightest bit, and asked her how she was, she might easily have disgraced herself; as it was, his terse politeness, bordering on coolness, had kept her rigidly in control. No one, except Dilys, knew about her split with Neil. Obviously she would have to make the news more widely known pretty soon, but just now it was Dilys and no one else, and although Dil loved to gossip she could keep her mouth shut where her closest friends were concerned. Dilys had surprised Charis by saying that she thought she had done the right thing.

'You've been looking peely-mealy for ages, and it wasn't only the weather, you were having doubts which you wouldn't face up to,' she told her.

'Tell Nurse Adams to sit with Mr Fellowes,' Sister called from the office doorway. 'I've given her his Kardex, but try and find out how much she's absorbed. She's a slow learner, is that one, she needs encouragement, and time spending on her too, which I'm afraid we haven't got. Still, see what you can do, Staff.' Sister Holt went back to her desk, wondering how on earth she would get through the next six weeks before she and her friend from Gynae went on leave.

Charis sat down at the Nurses' Station with young Jane Adams. 'Tell me what you know about the type of surgery Mr Fellowes has had, Nurse.' She took the patient's Kardex from her hand.

'He's had a laminectomy incision, Staff, part of his disc . . . the prolapsed intervertebral disc, has been taken out.'

'From between which vertebrae?'

'Numbers two and three lumbar, I think.'

'No, between three and four lumbar,' Charis pointed to the notes. 'Now, you helped me make up his bed this morning, so you know the type it is—an orthopaedic bed with a reinforced spring. He needs his spine supported, but not so rigidly as in a plaster. And tomorrow, believe it or not, he'll be having extension exercises, very gentle ones, and these will be increased daily, as his pain settles. That's fine, Jane, now go and sit with him, and when he wakes up again take his temperature, pulse, and respiration rate, and enter them on his chart.'

'Yes, Staff, thank you, Staff.' Off she went to bed number five. And she's not so slow as all that, Charis thought. Once she's got a thing it sticks. She hasn't got a butterfly mind like some, for all her gossamer looks—Jane Adams was a slender, light-footed platinum blonde.

Stopping only to speak to Mr Palfrey, who was sitting beside his bed, looking tree-trunk stiff in his plaster jacket, Charis made her way to the day room, where she knew she would find Mr William Ivyson.

William Ivyson was going home, as soon as his wife arrived. He too was in a plaster support, which he would need to wear for some time. Standing beside him was Guy Morland, tilting his long length against the table. 'Come in, Staff,' he beckoned as he saw Charis slow down, 'You're not intruding, I'm just off, I've a fracture clinic at two, but I couldn't go without saying goodbye to one of our long-staying patients . . . if not *the* longest!' he smiled at Mr Ivyson, who was sitting bolt upright on one of the hard-seated chairs.

'I was just saying to Mr Morland, Staff, how jittery I feel about leaving, which doesn't make sense, when all I've thought about, ever since I came in, was getting back home with my wife and family. I'm all of a shake . . . look at that!' Mr Ivyson held out his hands, which were trembling. Charis waded in with kind words.

'Patients who've been with us for a very long time often feel like that,' she assured him.

'We call it becoming institutionalized,' said Guy, backing her up. 'It can be quite a traumatic experience, leaving hospital. After a day or two at home, though, you'll know you're in your right place. The other will drop away like a shell, like your original plaster bed! Anyway, you're not done with us yet, we'll be meeting in Outpatients' Clinic. No doubt you'll have got your card with the first appointment date?'

'Yes, sir, safe and sound.'

'And as soon as we possibly can, we'll replace your plaster corset with a more flexible arrangement. Then after that, if all goes well, as I'm very sure it will, you'll need no support, you'll walk about a free man.'

Guy's eyes met Charis's, and they smiled at one another, each of them remembering, perhaps, an afternoon just before Christmas, when Sir Rodney Barks had prophesied that the then supine Mr Ivyson would be dancing on Trinity Green on May the first.

There are few things so reassuring as a shared smile, Charis thought, as she watched Guy Morland's white-coated back retreating to the doors. But oh, how he knows how to use his charm . . . a smile to draw you in, a frown and a baleful look, if it suits him to thrust you out again. He would be hell to fall in love with. To fall in love with G.M. would mean being bounced about like a ball, either thrown or caught, as he fancied. Was Joanne Tolbie as tough as he was, or didn't she mind the hassle of an up-and-down life?

Charis wished her joy of it.

CHAPTER SIX

No one had decided on Homer's fate, but Charis was determined to keep him. How she would do so in a flat, when at last she was able to buy one, she didn't know, but in no way was she going to part with him. Nan and Harold were cat-lovers; they had two black moggies who spat hate at every canine in sight. 'You and I must stick together, Homer,' Charis told him on Friday evening, when she got home and changed, and took him for his run.

They turned down College Walk, making for the river. Once there Homer was let off his leash, and he bounded across the meadows, his fringed mahogany legs standing hock-high in buttercups, as he stopped to investigate something in the grass. He was two years old and he hadn't as yet put aside puppy ways. He missed her father, Charis knew that by the way he behaved in the house—sticking very close to her side, raising a hopeful head when he heard a car slowing down in the lane. Neil had always made a fuss of him, so he probably missed Neil too. You and me both, thought Charis, trying not to see the couples walking along the towpath, sitting entwined on seats, lying locked together in the grass.

It was so strange not being one of a couple. She had known Neil for a long time, had been going about with him for a long time; suddenly not doing so had made a kind of vacuum in her life. She no longer wanted to marry him, of that she was perfectly sure, but she missed his steady companionship, even his fussy ways. When she was not on duty, there was loneliness of a kind.

As she came to the bridge just beyond the lock, she decided to cross over. She would walk along on the opposite bank. She might treat herself to a coffee at the Keats House Hotel, in their brand new Patio Bar. 'They allow dogs in there, I've seen them,' she told a panting Homer who, wildly excited, loped on to the bridge. It was a wooden bridge with a handrail, open at the sides. Charis saw no reason to leash him, for even if he fell in, which was very unlikely, he could swim like a dolphin; he had very often done so, in the summer months, when her father had brought him this way.

Perhaps because she was thinking of that, thinking back to happier times, she failed to notice the trio of boys catcalling from the opposite bank. They were bent on mischief, on doing damage, and they began throwing stones. The first one narrowly missed her face and flew on into the river, the second struck Homer on the head. He yelped, staggered and swayed, then keeled over on to his side and toppled off the bridge—to the sound of Charis screaming his name, to the sound of her running feet, to the shrill cry of 'Bullseye!' from one of the boys.

'Homer! Homer! Homer . . . *here!*' Charis shouted from the bank, but the spuming water was flattening out, was rippling away in folds, in ever-widening circles to lap against the reeds. There was no sign of a canine body plunging its way towards her. Not daring to waste a second more, she bent and tore off her shoes, then easing herself down into the water, catching her breath at its chill, she began to swim to the spot where Homer had gone in. She searched under water near the bridge; it was deep, six feet at least. Her clothes impeded her, so did the mud, which eddied up in spirals, clouding her vision, stinging her eyes. She closed them and broke surface, fighting and fighting against the weight of her clothes. Even then she trod water, still desperately searching, straining her eyes to see. He must be wedged, entangled in weeds, hurt . . . unconscious, perhaps. Not dead . . . not dead . . . oh, please, not dead! she thought desperately, I can't go home without him! She flattened her body and swam again, this time under the bridge . . . and then *she saw him,* out on the bank, shaking and flapping himself, a whirling flurry of water-spiked dark red hair . . .

'You fool dog!' She shouted at him, relief coursing through her like new life, as she got herself out through the mud and the reeds to his side. 'You fool dog!' She looked at him blearily, then rather more closely, as she saw the small wound on his forehead, just above his eye. It had probably stunned him, momentarily; it didn't look all that bad. But they'd have to get home . . . they couldn't stop here. She was shivering violently. Where were her shoes? She saw them, made herself move to get them. She put them on, and they filled with the water that was streaming off her jeans. Her thin woollen sweater clung like a skin. She pulled her hair forward and wrung it, twisted it round like a rope of sodden silk. Now, run . . . run . . . get home . . . be quick! She put Homer on his lead, and they set off, Charis pulled by the dog, pierced to the bone by the wind, which was only a breeze but cut like a keen-edged knife. Homer dragged at her arm . . . it might come off. Her teeth began to chatter.

She knew that people were turning to stare, as she reached the towpath area. She knew, and she didn't care, because she was going to freeze to death; her legs were slimy mud to the knees, her feet made a squelching sound. She reached College Walk, but by then she was almost running along in a daze. It was no small wonder that, dragged by Homer, she nearly ran into a car that was turning into the forecourt of

Mayfield Flats. It stopped, and she ran behind its chassis, feeling, for a second, the puff of exhaust pipe warmth on her legs, and then she felt something else—a descending hand on her shoulder, Homer's lead prised from her hand, herself being pushed and urged into the flats by a voice she recognised: Guy Morland's voice, forceful, bossy. She was too cold to protest, too cold to protest or worry . . . let it all happen, she thought. They were in a lift, they were getting out, Homer was shaking himself. Charis heard the scrape of a key in a lock, the sift of a door grazing back. Then came a warm interior, carpets under her feet, pale walls, light paint. 'The mess—I'm all mud! And my dog . . . I can't . . . ' juddered from her lips.

'In here!' He propelled her towards a bathroom, pressed her down on a stool. He gave her a swift assessing look, then took his hand from her shoulder. 'Strip off,' he said tersely, 'and get under that shower. Leave your clothes on the floor. I'll dig out some dry ones—and yes, yes,' he saw her glance at her dog, 'I'll see to him. Now do as I say.' He went out, closing the door. 'I shan't disturb you,' he called back, and she heard him talking to Homer, as she peeled off her clothes and found the right taps to turn.

Nothing had ever been quite so blissful, so wonderful as that shower—needles of warmth hitting her skin, sliving through her hair, bouncing off her upturned face, beating down on her feet. She found soap in the rack, she lathered and rinsed; nothing in the world could compare with this feeling of warmth and cleanliness. The rough masculine towel she dried on was all that was needed to bring her back to normal reasoning. Heavens above, what about her clothes? She stared at the heap on the floor—a tiled floor, and thank goodness it was—but even so, what a mess! She wound the towel about her and bent to pick them up, just as a tap came on the door; she called out a laughing 'Come

in'. To laugh the situation off was the only thing to
do, but Guy marched in, straight-faced and efficient,
one arm hung about with clothes, his free hand
clutching a plastic bag.

'Put your clothes in the bag, and wear these dry
ones; they should at least keep you warm.'

She took them from him. 'I'm sure they will,' she
managed to laugh again, but embarrassment swept
her, and she couldn't look at him.

'Come out when you're ready.' He backed to the
door. 'I'll make a pot of tea, and while you're drinking
it you can tell me how you landed yourself in this
mess.'

He went out looking irritated, which Charis felt
sure he was. She had obviously disrupted his evening,
and what was even worse, in order to get rid of her
he would have to drive her home. She could hardly
walk the quarter-mile from the flats to Cranleigh
House arrayed in his clothes; she began to put them
on. There was a cotton shirt, which came to her knees
and gave her the armless look of a Venus de Milo,
until she rolled up the sleeves. There was a pair of
socks, which she pulled up like boots, and a blue
towelling bathrobe, short on Guy, she was quite sure,
but full length on herself. There was a comb in the
pocket, so she did her hair, smoothing the clean damp
tresses away from her face and down her centre back.
Then, shuffling a little, and taking care in case she
tripped up on his socks, she left the bathroom and
crossed the strip of hall.

Just before she entered the sitting-room she glimpsed
the scene inside it—the stretch of green carpet, the
glowing gas-fire, Homer in front of it, steaming like a
blanket, sitting sentinel-straight, looking at the man
who had just dressed his wound and made a good job
of it. Last but not least, she saw Guy Morland, black
hair falling forward, directing a stream of tea into two
hefty mugs. When he saw her he drew her towards

the fire, smiling hospitably. 'Well, my bathrobe's never looked so splendid!' He was making her feel at ease, or trying to. She sank down into a chair. 'How are you feeling?' He watched the red setter leaning against her legs.

'As though you've saved my life,' she smiled.

'This will add the finishing touch.' He passed her one of the steaming mugs, and she held it between her hands. As she sipped from it she tasted whisky, but she made no comment on this. It was a hot toddy and the right medicine. She was warm inside and out before she had got halfway down the mug.

'And now,' said Guy, no doubt assuming he had timed the moment just right, 'you can tell me what happened to you . . . what happened to you both. I've dressed Homer's cut, by the way, it should heal in a couple of days. He's not hurt anywhere else, I've had a good look at him.'

'Thank you. I'm grateful, and I know he is.'

'Never mind about that. What happened, Charis?' His voice sharpened. 'How did you get in the river? Was there someone fooling about, did you miss your footing? Did you tumble in?'

'None of those. Well, actually, there *was* someone fooling about—a group of boys, three of them. They began throwing stones when Homer and I were crossing the bridge just beyond the lock . . . '

'Throwing stones *at* you!'

She nodded. 'And Homer was hit.' She went on with her story and told it to the end. 'And I think,' she added, as she finished her drink, 'that he must have been stunned by the stone, but that the icy water brought him round, perhaps washed him up near the bank. He must have been lying there spewing up water, all the time I was searching for him.'

'Blasted kids!' Guy burst out. 'They want a damn good hiding!'

I agree, but you'd have to catch them first. There

was no sight nor sound of them, after I clambered out,' she explained.

'And what *you* did was foolhardy!' He turned his anger on her. 'Plunging in like that, staying in . . . swimming around all that time. Have you no thought for your . . . your *wellbeing?* Are you *asking* to be ill? River water in early spring has winter under its crust!'

'So I noticed!' Charis retorted. Need he be quite so rude? Need he be quite so lecturing? Had he no idea at all of what she had felt like when Homer disappeared? And was foolhardy the same as foolish? She had a vague idea that 'foolhardy' meant 'foolishly rash'; if so he was probably right. She had been accused, often enough, of being exactly that.

And all this didn't endear him to her, the more so because she could hardly retaliate and be rude in return, not when she was in his flat, a sort of guest, and sitting in his clothes. 'I'm sure the drink you have given me will ward off any ills,' she said, trying to rise from the chair with some semblance of dignity. 'And thank you for all your other help, but I ought to be getting home.'

'So soon?' he said, and he took the mug from her, watching her and waiting . . . waiting for what he knew only too well she was going to *have* to ask. He was taking pleasure in it too. How detestable he was!

'Mr Morland,' she began, 'I've disturbed your evening, and I'm very sorry about it, but unfortunately I have to ask you one last favour. Can you, I wonder, possibly run me home?'

'For heaven's sake, of course I'll take you! I fully intended to.' His reassurance came swiftly enough, but only, she felt, in words. His manner was at variance with what he said, he still looked irritated. 'You could hardly come out in my bathrobe, either. I'll fetch you a mackintosh—you can button it up from neck to hem.' He ushered her from the room, or rather shooed her out of it, into the narrow hall. 'There's your bag of wet clothes, the dog's leash, and this is the mackintosh.' He helped her into the latter, still issuing commands. 'I'll bring the car round as near to the main doors as possible. When I sound the horn, make for the lift and streak down and join me.'

If he had his way he'd do me up with brown paper and string, and deliver me by mail van! Charis told a prancing Homer. She delved into the plastic bag and found her front door key in the small back pocket of her soused-with-water jeans. Thank goodness the pocket had been zipped up; how awful it would have been to have arrived at Cranleigh with no means of getting in!

The short journey was made without mishap, and with little conversation. Homer swayed on the back seat, going crazy with excitement when they reached the house and got out on the gravel sweep. 'If you'd like to come in for a few minutes,' Charis said to Guy Morland, 'I can do a quick change and give you back your clothes.'

'What a good idea,' he said pleasantly. He was looking at the house. He liked its setting, the attractive garden, dotted about with shrubs, tulips in bud round the bowls of the trees, wallflowers in profusion, a stretch of lawn, a glossy-leafed laurel hedge. 'May I walk through and see the back garden?' He followed a shuffling Charis, still in his socks and crackling mac, into the spacious hall.

'Of course . . . through the kitchen,' she pointed it out, then crackled upstairs to change. Pulling on briefs and cords and shirt, and standing well back from the window, she watched him crossing the back lawn, saw him stop to inspect the rockery, squat on his heels and finger a tiny plant. 'The Surgeon who likes Gardens' would be a perfect caption for a sketch of him in that particular pose. Charis sighed a little as she folded his clothes and wrapped them in tissue paper. Guy Morland made her nervous, but *why?* She wasn't a nervous type; she was rarely shy of anyone, didn't mind what people thought . . . well, not over-much . . . and men usually liked her. She felt he did not. So was that at the root of it all? Did she see him as a challenge? Was she trying to find favour in his eyes, make him change his opinion of her? If so, what a daft and hopeless goal to try to achieve. She crossed the landing and began to descend the stairs.

She was halfway down them when she saw him coming in through the kitchen entrance, looking about him with that head-in-the-air, all-seeing manner of his. She expected him to ask what most people did—was she living there all on her own? But no such question passed his lips . . . trust him to be different! He was smiling at her, looking up at her; she was four stairs from the bottom. In her haste not to keep him waiting, and keeping her eyes on his face, she did that heart-stopping, terrifying thing—stepped out into mid-air, thinking she had reached the bottom of the flight.

There was a second of knowing . . . of falling, of dropping, then hands were gripping her waist, she was tipped towards a startled Guy Morland, who held her fast against him, her feet trailing an inch from the floor, his voice tickling her ear. 'You must be *trying* to scare me half to death, Charis Littleton!' She couldn't move, didn't want to move, she only moved when he did, when he turned his face, when she knew he would kiss her, when he did so . . . and did so . . . and did so; when she kissed him back with all her strength, with everything that was in her . . . when the world stopped turning, then moved on the other way.

'Pleasant though that was, it shouldn't have happened,' she heard as her feet touched the floor, as his arms left her and she saw his face in proper perspective once more. His eyes gleamed black between his lashes, his facial lines were carved, but his mouth smiled imperturbably enough, and she felt a sense of outrage that he could stand there like that, so unaffected, could flick off so much feeling with easy composure . . . and call it *pleasant,* and half apologise.

'Put it down to shock reaction,' she made herself smile back. 'It's not every day you have a female hurtling down from a great height. It's not every day I throw myself into a man's arms, either!' She managed to laugh, but not very convincingly. The tissue paper parcel of clothes lay on the bottom stair and she bent to retrieve it. 'Don't forget what you were waiting for.' She was starting to shake, to tremble all over, and she prayed he wouldn't notice. She practically willed him to turn away, which he did, just as they heard the sound of car tyres crushing the gravel outside. 'That sounds like Neil!' She stared at the door.

'I expect it is, don't you?' Guy mistook her surprise for alarm. 'Relax, Charis,' he said, 'forget our little fall from grace. So far as I'm concerned, it never happened, and won't again. Now go and let him in, and let me out.' He looked gravely down at her.

The bell shrilled as she opened the door. Neil was on the step, smiling his anxious, closed smile, blinking behind his glasses, wearing the vulnerable look that had always made her want to annihilate anyone who tried to do him down. 'I've brought you a present!' he dangled a tiny string-threaded bag from his finger, then he saw Guy coming out, and stood back to let him pass. 'Sorry, I didn't realise . . . ' he began, but Guy waved a peremptory hand.

'I'm going, don't worry.' Off he went, raising his hand once more before he slid into the car and drove away.

'I saw his car, but I thought it was Nan's,' said Neil, shutting the door.

'Yes, I know, it's very like hers. Neil, why have you

come?' Charis asked quickly, leading the way into the sitting-room.

'To bring you this.' The little bag was put into her hands. 'Your father's room at the office is being cleared for redecoration. I found that, 'he stabbed at the bag, 'inside a roll of plans. I knew you'd given it to him, so I thought you might like to have it.' He watched as she widened the bag and drew out a global glass paperweight. It had a country scene inside it—a ploughed field and a tractor, a minuscule man on the tractor seat, white gulls following. The top of the globe was the bowl of the sky; it was cleverly, beautifully fashioned. Charis had bought it for her father from the Glass Mountain Shop in Kingsford, just over a year ago. 'I thought you might like to have it,' Neil repeated, sitting down. He couldn't tell what she was thinking, her hair was screening her face. He had come here with a purpose in mind, but seeing Morland with her had thrown him off course . . . surely she hadn't taken up with someone else? He turned his attention to Homer, who was fawningly pleased to see him. He fondled his ears, then saw the small abrasion above his eye. He wondered what had happened, then suddenly Charis was speaking, looking across, and shaking back her hair.

'Thank you, Neil, I'd love to have it. Thank you for bringing it round. It was thoughtful of you.' She cradled the globe in her hands.

'That's all right, I'm glad you're pleased.' He took off his glasses and cleaned them. There was so much he wanted to say to her, but he didn't know how to begin, so he started with Homer. 'He seems to have hurt his head.'

'Yes, poor old boy!' She told him about it, and of Guy Morland's part in it all. She half expected frowning looks and disapproving noises, but all Neil said . . . and cheerfully too . . . was: 'Good job it wasn't worse.' She could only suppose that freed from the chains of being engaged to her, he felt no need to change her attitudes. Given time we could meet as friends, she thought, with no stresses or strains. With some men friendship would never be possible; her mind filled with Guy Morland. Quickly she asked Neil how life at the office was.

'Not good, not bad.' He spread out his hands, 'so-so, I think you'd say. Margaret Brodie is back in a fortnight's time, but what will happen then is anyone's guess. I can't see there'll be any position for her. And she still doesn't know your father has died . . . that's what's so terrible.

'You can't help that.'

He blinked at her. The fact that she had said 'you' and not 'we' didn't escape his notice. She hadn't taken long to dissociate herself from all his concerns and cares. He had been going to suggest, when he set out this evening, that she might like to meet him occasionally. He had been going to put it carefully, but timing was important, and this was the wrong time; he saw that clearly. Give it another week, he told himself, getting up to go.

'There's no ill-feeling between us, is there?' was all he ventured to ask.

'Of course not, Neil . . . none,' Charis assured him. She went out with him to the car. In a bid to establish good faith, or to recreate old times, he remembered to give a pip on his horn when he turned out into the lane.

Yet even Neil, not too well endowed with sensitivity, hadn't failed to notice how far away Charis had seemed.

CHAPTER SEVEN

HE saw her next, by chance, on Tuesday, just before one o'clock. She was going on duty—the late shift —and was wheeling her bicycle down Princes Parade towards the Hospital gates. He was on the other side of the road; they waved through a welter of traffic, then moved on, each going their separate ways.

'Your fiancé was in seeing Mr Trueman on Sunday afternoon,' Peggy Barford told Charis, as they tidied beds, before the start of visiting. 'Still, you'll have seen him since, so you'll know.' Charis had been on days off.

'Actually, Peggy, Neil and I are no longer engaged,' she said, deciding that now was as good a time as any to make things plain. 'We broke it off the week before last. We felt it was for the best. I ought to have told you before this, but—well, you know how it is.'

Peggy didn't. At twenty-two she was very happily married, with a baby boy of ten months, looked after by her mother, but she managed to say all the right things, and tactfully swerved the talk by telling Charis that Melissa Ivyson was still seeing Peter Trueman, even though her father had been discharged.

'Peter doesn't lack for visitors.' Charis straightened a sheet, but she was thinking more of Neil's visitation rather than Melissa's. Of course, Neil did *know* Mr Trueman, through working next door to him. Hanson & Sons, and Mathieson & Pratt shared the same set of railings, the same neat privet hedge at the back. She knew they had sometimes lunched together; they were roughly the same age. So what could be more

natural than for Neil to visit him? Nothing at all . . .
she dismissed it from her mind. What she couldn't
dismiss quite so readily was the thought that Guy
Morland might, for some reason, come on to the
ward, and looking him in the eye was going to be
extremely difficult. The only way I can do it is by
pretending that last Friday never happened, she told
herself. I'll pretend it was a dream. So really the
sooner he comes and gets it over with, the better, she
reasoned, as she made her way down the ward.

The first batch of visitors had come, she could see
them in the corridor, where they had to wait till the
doors were pulled back at two-thirty sharp. No patient
was supposed to have more than two visitors at a
time, but if there were no serious cases in the ward,
or no immediate post-ops, the nurse in charge turned
a blind eye during the last ten minutes, when there
could be double that number round some of the beds.

The central sterile supplies department had rung up
for the stock level sheets. Charis went to the office to
complete them—a boring but necessary job. From
time to time she glanced through the viewing window
into the ward, keeping an eye on the patients rather
than on their visitors. The usual miscellany of gifts
lay around on beds, and bed-tables and lockers-
—sweets, fruit, bottles of squash, books and magazines.
There were one or two offerings of flowers, shop-
wrapped in cornet-shaped bags, but these were in the
minority; male patients weren't often brought flowers.
Female Orthopaedic next door, where Dilys Hughes
worked, was the one that resembled a floral bower at
times.

Melissa had brought Peter Trueman a jigsaw.
Sensible girl, Charis thought. It would relax him, yet
keep his brain agile . . . no one could read all day.
It would be another two to three weeks before Peter
could bear any weight on his injured leg, which was
taking its time to heal. The stitches had been removed

from his arm—the plaster having been sprung, then
reinstated afterwards, much to his annoyance. 'It feels
as though it's in irons, not plaster,' he was telling
Melissa. She was holding his hand and telling him not
to moan.

Charis went into the ward herself, and chatted to
one or two relatives. Mr Palfrey had his son with
him—a florid-faced, thickset man, with a bullet head,
and the start of an early paunch. He wanted to know
when his father would be out. Charis parried the
question.

'You'll have to ask Mr Morland that.'

'Never see him, do I? I've never set eyes on any top
brass, not once, all the times I've been here. Seems to
me they make themselves scarce in case they're asked
too many questions.'

'Not always, Mr Palfrey . . . I *am* speaking to
Mr Palfrey junior?' Guy Morland enquired as he
neared the foot of the bed.

Charis performed the introductions, hoping her face
showed none of the shock she felt at his unheralded
appearance. With her back to the doors, and with so
many people in the ward, she had had no warning of
his approach. As the three men began to talk together,
she excused herself and left. If he wanted her she
would be in the office; he would know that, and come
there . . . which was what he did about ten minutes
afterwards.

'No ill effects from your dip, Staff?' he enquired
from the doorway. There was nothing in his face to
embarrass her, his look was unrevealing—not friendly,
not hostile, just neutral. I might be the *paperboy*, she
thought with a surge of feeling that she couldn't
identify.

'No ill effects at all,' she said stiffly.

He came further into the room. 'I wanted a word
with Sister Holt.'

'She'll be here tomorrow morning.' She didn't ask

him if she could help, just remained politely standing, till after a second or two of what appeared to be very deep thought, he thanked her curtly and went out, closing the door.

Charis shut her eyes, pressing her hands on either side of her face. Well, that was over, and thank goodness it was; next time would be easier. What a fuss and drama I'm making of it, she thought; anyone would think I'd never been kissed by a good-looking male ever before in my life! Taking herself to task worked wonders; she smiled brightly at Nurse Varden, who was coming in, bearing a tray of tea. 'Is it teatime already?' She took the tray.

'Yes, Staff, just on four.'

'Well, as soon as the visitors start to go, clear up in the ward. Mr Kahn and Mr Merridew and the bunionectomy patient can go through into the day room to play chess, if they like. That'll give you a chance to change their sheets—get Nurse Adams to help you.'

'Yes, Staff.' Nurse Varden went out. Charis drank her tea, then made a start on yet another pile of paperwork. She could hear the visitors leaving, hear footsteps passing her door. After that there were minutes of comparative quiet, then came different sounds—doors opening and shutting, cisterns flushing, the squeak of wheelchair tyres, the shifting thud of a walking-frame, the bonk of a stirrup iron, the impump, imp-ump of a patient walking with crutches, the caw of a cough, the sound of a raucous sneeze. A relative telephoned, asking how Mr Fellowes was getting on. She gave her name and asked Charis to let him know she had rung. 'Of course I will, I'll tell him now.' Charis went in the ward to do so, which was how she came to notice, with a good deal of surprise, that Melissa Ivyson was still there, and so was someone else, someone else at Peter Trueman's bed, an unknown dark-haired woman in a short leather skirt no wider than a tube. She was standing up and quarrelling—vi-

olently, it seemed—with Melissa, who was sitting on
the other side of the bed. Melissa was answering back,
and the noise and disturbance was considerable.
Ambulant patients were turning round . . . anything
out of the ordinary was meat and drink to men on a
long-staying ward.

'Visiting time finished ten minutes ago. I shall have
to ask you to leave.' Charis reached them at speed,
and raised her voice in order to make herself heard.

'I'll go when *she* does. If she stays, I do!' The girl
with the fierce black fringe glared at her while pointing
an arm over the bed at Melissa.

'Will you *both leave now*?' said Charis. Neither girl
moved an inch.

'Please do as Staff says.' Peter Trueman, in his rôle
of pig-in-the-middle, was looking upset and trembling
visibly. It was this that made Charis take a tougher
line. She moved to the head of the bed.

'I'm sorry, but if you persist in staying, I shall have
to ring down to Security. That'll mean you'll be taken
forcibly from the ward, right down to the yard, across
it and out of the hospital gates!'

'Could be I'd enjoy that!' The dark-haired girl gave
a laugh. She had sharp features, a sharp hairstyle, she
looked spiteful, vixenish. What she did next seemed
to prove that she was. Giving Charis a shove, she
flashed round the bed, grasped Melissa's chair, and
tipped her out of it, with one quick vicious jerk of her
arms. As Melissa hit the floor, as she sprawled on the
vinyl, half under the bed, the girl shouted: 'That'll
teach you to sit and drool over Pete! Find a man of
your own . . . you're old enough!' She spun round
on a pin-narrow heel, and crashed into the hard,
unyielding front of Guy Morland, who had heard the
noise from the corridor outside.

'Shall we make our way out?' he enquired pleasantly, pointing to the door. Perhaps bemused by his
looks and charm, or quelled by the steel in his voice,

she muttered a sullen, 'Okay,' and left, Guy an inch behind her. He made quite sure she left the premises.

Charis and Nurse Varden helped Melissa up. She was all right, she said. She assured Peter of this, as she bent and kissed him goodbye. He just kept saying, 'I'm sorry, I'm sorry,' over and over again. It was perfectly obvious, too, that Melissa was very far from all right. She was holding her wrist and her face was paste-white. Charis got her out of the ward and into the office and into a chair just in time, for there she fainted, dropping forward like a rag doll.

She was surfacing by the time Guy returned. Charis had known he would come. He would want to know what was going on, what had sparked off the row, but just at the moment his concern, like hers, was all for the girl in the chair. 'Exactly where is the pain, Miss Ivyson?' Gently lifting her arm, he placed it on the arm of the chair. 'Can you move your fingers at all?' She did so, and winced. He smiled in sympathy.

'You may have fractured your wrist. We'll get you to X-Ray.' He moved to the phone. 'I'll ring down and tell them you're on your way. We'll jump the queue, if we can. Fix her up with a sling, Staff, get her taken down in a chair.'

'I can walk. I'm not hurt anywhere else—it was just the shock, that's all. I had no idea . . . I didn't know . . . ' Melissa broke off, on the brink of tears, as Charis knotted the sling about her neck. When the wheelchair arrived, brought by Nurse Varden, she climbed in without argument. Charis and Guy watched her wheeled away to the lifts.

Guy was screwing up his eyes as he sometimes did when perplexed. 'Staff Nurse, tell me,' he shut the door, 'wasn't it playing with fire to allow Trueman's ex-wife to go into the ward, when Miss Ivyson was there, probably holding his hand?'

'His ex-wife!' Charis stared.

'Well, that's what she said. She's been working

abroad, so had only just heard about his accident. She told me that she gave you her name, and you let her go into the ward.'

'Did she indeed!' This was so untrue, it wasn't worth contradicting. 'Ex-wife or not, she's a spiteful woman,' Charis managed at last. '*If* I had known who she was, and *if* I had seen her outside the ward, I'd have stopped her going in—at least until I'd spoken to Peter. I don't apply matches to explosive situations if I can possibly help it. I don't believe she *is* his ex-wife. I think she's his ex-live-in girl-friend, hoping to slot back into his life!'

'Good thinking! It matches my own. That's precisely what I thought,' said Guy. When she saw him smile she could hardly believe it; she had expected more criticism, and blame too, for what had occurred in the ward.

'Well, thank you. I thought . . . '

'We do on occasion think alike, don't we, Staff?' His look, or glance—it was no more than that—was plainly one of approval. It smoothed her ruffled feelings and feathers, made her feel at one with him, made it possible for her to say she was sorry.

'I feel dreadful about it, you know.'

'Not your fault.' He reached for the door, just as she made to do so. They brushed hands and the fleeting contact jarred Charis from top to toe. Instantly the scene on the stairs at Cranleigh last Friday swept into her mind with so much force, so much realism, that she felt he was holding her close, all over again.

There was a stillness about him, a waiting second, and then he opened the door. 'Come on,' he said, 'let's see how Trueman has survived being fought over!' And his 'let's see' struck the right note, it paired her with him professionally; they were working together in doctor/nurse partnership.

Mr Palfrey was talking to Peter Trueman—he *would* be, of course. Peter looked as though, more than anything else, he could use a good stiff drink. 'Is Lissa all right?' he asked them. 'I know she said she was, but she looked very pale, and of course she was shocked. If only I could have explained!'

'I think she may have a broken wrist,' Guy said quietly. 'She's on her way to X-Ray now, Nurse Barford has taken her.'

'Oh, no! How awful!' Peter Trueman looked upset. 'Will she have to stay in?'

'Not a chance! Her wrist will be set under local anaesthesia, she'll have a split plaster applied, then a car will take her home.'

'You *do* think it's broken, then?'

'I'm pretty sure it is.' Guy sat on the edge of the bed, his all-seeing eye doing a quick assessment of the patient's condition, after all the fuss and fisticuffs. 'Keep the others away from him,' was his quiet aside to Charis. He meant the walking patients, like Mr Donald Palfrey, who were all agog to get the inside news.

Out in the office he explained how it was he had chanced to be in the ward just in time to escort the aggressive female to the doors. 'I was coming along to bring this,' he handed over a folder. 'It's the case history of a new patient who's being admitted on Thursday. I intended to bring it for Sister tomorrow, but it struck me you might like a preview. The patient is a schoolmaster, name of Giles Barry, had polio as a child. He's had trouble with his right leg ever since, wore a caliper for years. The condition has worsened in that the hip slips out at frequent intervals. As he's only thirty Sir Rodney considered, and I agree with him, that he's not a suitable candidate for a hip replacement job. We've both seen him in Outpatients, we've talked with him and his wife; the result being that Sir Rodney will do a Chiari osteotomy.'

'So he'll be in a hip spica?'

'For about a month . . . yes, he will, a one and a

half hip spica, immediately following surgery. He'll be transferred from the operating table straight on to a turning bed. It'll be a long job, and he's going to be a heavy nursing case.'

'But well worth it,' Charis observed, 'if, at the end of it all, Mr Barry can walk without all these falls,' she was doing a scan of the notes.

'Yes, he's been having a bad time, poor chap; in fact he now admits that he feels the hip is dislocated virtually all the time. He obviously can't . . . ' Guy broke off as the door opened a crack, then widened to admit Joanne Tolbie, dressed for going out, in a tangerine raincoat cut with such flair that it seemed to the staring Charis as though she had stepped straight off the cover of *Vogue*. Her hair was the sort that was curly all over, it fell in a cloud to her shoulders; her eyes were dark, and they looked at the man by the desk.

'So this is where you're hiding! I thought we were going out.' She walked the three of four paces that brought her to his side.

'We are. I've just finished, I'm coming right now.' The telephone rang on the desk. It was answered by Charis, who passed it to him.

'It's for you, from A and E.'

'About Miss Ivyson, no doubt.' He took the receiver and carried it to the window, talking all the time.

Joanne engaged Charis in conversation, telling her that boy triplets had been born by Caesarean section down in Maternity Block. 'I've just been to see them, they're gorgeous, all in incubators, of course. You could go, if you wanted to, but you'd have to be gowned up.'

Charis heard Guy replace the phone, so did Joanne, who swung round to face him. 'I was just telling Charis about the triplets.' She turned back to Charis. 'You really should go and see them, Charis, that is if you're interested. You'll probably be having your own babies before very long, but I don't suppose you want them in threes! I'm quite sure I wouldn't, either!' she laughed, looking straight at Guy, whose expression didn't change.

'Neil and I,' Charis said quickly, 'have decided not to marry. We're no longer engaged.' She disliked explaining with Guy standing there. She was aware of him staring, she heard his arm shift as he plunged it into his pocket. She kept her eyes rigidly fixed on Joanne, willing her to be tactful, to simply say, 'Sorry' or 'Oh dear,' and leave it at that. Her pencil-slim brows rose high at the news.

'Oh, Charis, but *why*?' she exclaimed. 'You're so well suited, Neil's so attractive . . . you make such a . . . very good pair!'

'People are allowed to have second thoughts, Jo,' Guy's voice cut across hers. 'Now, if I could just get a word in edgeways and give a message to Staff.'

'Oh, sorry, sorry! Carry on!' Joanne feigned fear of him, standing back and flattening against the wall.

He removed his white coat and hung it over his arm. 'The Ivyson girl,' he told Charis, 'is having her wrist reduced in Minor Ops right at this moment; the film showed a Colles' break. She'll be going home in about an hour. Could you see her before she goes? It would set Trueman's mind at rest, I think. He's in quite a state, poor chap.'

'Yes, of course I'll see her,' said Charis, snatching at the chance to get back to ward matters, and off the subject of Neil. 'I'll tell Peter Trueman I'm going too, he may want to send a message.'

'Good idea, many thanks.' Guy's smile included Joanne. 'And now I think I'm free to go, and I'm not sorry either. It's been what you might call a day and a half, chockfull of surprises. Goodnight then, Staff, we'll remove ourselves!' He let Joanne go out first, followed her, then leaned back in to close the office door. He didn't look at Charis again; his profile, shoulder and arm were all she saw before the door clicked to.

She sat at the desk for a full minute after he had gone. In a way he had taken her part just now; he had silenced Joanne Tolbie, when without his intervention she might have gone on about Neil. Sister Tolbie wasn't renowned for her tact, Charis remembered hearing that said. But perhaps one didn't need to be tactful when working in Theatre—just hyperefficient, dedicated and loyal, all of which Joanne was. She was also beautiful—peachy, vibrant—a smouldering type, Neil had called her. Presumably Guy and she were lovers. At that point of conjecture Charis got up from her chair and went into the ward.

Peggy Barford and Nurse Varden were doing four-hourly TPRs, Nurse Adams was at the central desk, Nurse Joiner was tidying beds. It wouldn't be very long before the supper trolleys were down. One or two of the bed-tables had been swung into position, while the table in the day room had been laid up with knives and forks. Some of the more able walking patients liked to help with these jobs, when they could. They were a decent crowd on the whole, thought Charis, and they had left Peter Trueman in peace, not pulled his leg, and taken the mickey, as Guy had feared they would. 'How is Lissa? Was her wrist broken? How is she now?' he asked, using his monkey pole to shift himself up in the bed.

Charis pulled up a chair and sat down beside him. 'Yes, her wrist *was* broken,' she said. 'It's being set now, in Minor Ops, and she's absolutely fine. As soon as supper is over, I'm going to slip down and see her. She's likely to be going home around seven o'clock or just after. If you've any message you'd like to send her, you can do it via me . . . write a note if you'd rather.'

'And she *is* okay?'

'I promise you, she is.'

'I'll write a note, then—yes, that'll be best.' His long, thin face brightened a little, then as quickly sobered. 'It was awful, wasn't it? I had no idea Claire would come in to see me, I didn't expect that at all. She's an old friend, she's been working in Brussels, she's been there nearly a year. She's an interpreter, speaks three different languages—she's a very brainy girl.'

It was a pity she hadn't been clever enough to learn to control her temper, Charis thought, but didn't say so. All she asked Peter was, did he want to see her should she come to the ward again? 'If a patient doesn't want a certain visitor, we can always protect him, providing that *we know about it*,' she made that emphasis.

He smiled faintly, moving his splinted arm across the bed. 'Thank you, Staff, I'll think about it.' His eyes avoided hers. Sensing his reluctance to discuss the matter further, she gave him his writing materials and left the bed.

Once suppers had been given out, she went down to the Accident Wing. Melissa was sitting in a wheelchair, waiting for transport to take her home. Her left arm, supported in a sling, was in plaster from knuckles to elbow. One of the nurses had made her a cup of tea.

She seemed pleased to get the note from Peter, and read it as she sat there, her plump young face doubling at the chin. 'Tell him it's all right, will you, Staff?' She put the note back in its envelope, using one hand, just as a nurse came to give her her Outpatients' card. A minute later her car arrived, and the driver took charge of her. 'It will probably all end very romantically, 'Peggy Barford said, back in the ward. 'She'll be in to see him tomorrow, I bet, and they'll have something else in common—a plastered arm each, and what could be better than that!'

It was ten o'clock when Charis went home, cycling

under the lamps down Silver Street, into College Walk, then left up Challoners Lane. The house stood in darkness at the end of the drive, but as soon as her wheels hit the gravel, she heard Homer's joyous bay of greeting, saw the sway of his head and shoulders in blurred outline behind the hall windowpane.

When she stepped inside there he was, standing on his hind legs, paws up on her shoulders, panting into her face. The cut on his head, as Guy said it would, was healing very nicely. 'You were lucky,' she told him, 'to have the attention of such an eminent surgeon.'

Joanne Tolbie, most likely at this very minute, was having all his attention . . . his personal attention; and once again, for the second time that day, Charis was forced to harness her thoughts and drive them, galloping fast, in another direction that didn't lead to Guy.

CHAPTER EIGHT

SHE ran into him two days later on Level Ten of the tower block—the Maternity and Baby Unit floor. Charis had been longing to see the triplets ever since Joanne Tolbie had told her about their birth on Tuesday night. Guy Morland, talking to the staff nurse in charge, was peering into the incubators. He was gowned up, as Charis was; he looked at her over his mask. 'I was pressured into coming,' he told her, 'and I always do as I'm told!'

'Whereas I've come of my own free will,' she smiled, capturing his mood, which appeared to be one of lightness and brightness on this gorgeous April evening. Sunshine was streaming into the ward.

'No one could call them beautiful, could they?' He bent forward to look more closely at the first child, called Jeremy; his name was tagged to his wrist.

'A woman could,' Charis was quick to say, and the staff nurse agreed with her. The babies, weighing less than four pounds apiece, were lying on their fronts. They were being nursed naked in their separate boxes; their legs and arms were flexed and drawn up on either side of their bodies, their heads were turned to the side. Two had hair, rather sparse dark hair, the third one was bald; they were all three deep in the Land of Nod.

'They're perfect little boys,' the nurse smiled, 'and their mother is doing fine. She's been up and walking about the main ward, and through here to see them. She and her husband are thrilled to bits, and dying to get them home—which won't be yet awhile, of course;

they have weight to put on yet.' She moved to the long window and adjusted the slatted blind. It would never do for the incubators to stand in direct sunlight, which would affect the controlled atmosphere inside.

Charis and Guy left the unit together, sharing the lift that ticked them through nine consecutive floors, down to the Accident Wing. 'My brother has twin daughters,' he said, as they reached the yard. 'They're teenagers now—fifteen; not a scrap alike. One is a poppet, the other a brat. Still, that's the way it goes. The incidence of triplets is much more rare. It only occurs, I think, once in every six thousand, four hundred pregnancies.'

'Twins would be rather fun, I think, but triplets one too many!' laughed Charis, fastening her cape with the cross-over scarlet straps, leaving the collar button undone. The evening was warm, the breeze balmy; she breathed it in deeply.

'Are you off duty now? Are you going home?' he asked, as they reached the turning that led to the laundries and the brick-built bicycle sheds.

'Yes, but I haven't got my cycle, the front tyre's punctured,' she told him quickly, and edged away, because she didn't want him to think she was putting out feelers for a lift. But perhaps that was what he did think, for, looking straight ahead, then staring up at the sky, as though counting the number of clouds, he informed her that his car had gone in for an overhaul.

'Not,' he added, 'that I mind walking. It's my favourite exercise.'

'I quite enjoy it myself,' she said, turning towards the gates. And he didn't suggest accompanying her, just kept on doing so, steering her adroitly across Princes Parade and into Silver Street. They talked about Hospital matters at first, but when they got to the bridge they stopped there, by mutual accord, leaning over the parapet, enjoying the sunshine, the smell of the river, and rejoicing in the sight of St Saviour's College Chapel in all its majesty, thrusting its pale pinnacles into the light.

'I was very surprised to hear about your broken engagement,' he remarked. Somehow or other the atmosphere, the soft evening ambience, made a remark of this nature not too impossible.

'Several people were, including my sister.' Charis leaned farther over the bridge, watching a swan bending his neck in a long white question mark.

'Charis, I have to ask you this,' he touched her shoulder and turned her, looking down at her, making her look at him. 'I hope the break wasn't brought about by last Friday's happenings—by my bringing you home, and being in evidence, when Chambers came round to see you. If it was, I can put things right with him, perfectly easily. I'd hate to think . . . '

'Then don't,' she said quickly, 'because that wasn't the case at all. We decided not to get married just over a week ago . . . long before I plunged in the river, and before you dried me out and brought me home in borrowed clothes.' And kissed me on the stairs, she could have added, and nearly did. And perhaps Guy read her mind, for he said every bit as quickly as she:

'I'm glad I wasn't the cause, that I didn't precipitate a quarrel through some sort of misunderstanding.'

'You had nothing to do with it, Neil and I didn't quarrel, we just simply reached a decision. There's certainly no ill-feeling, and we're certainly not estranged.'

'Obviously not, as he still comes to see you!' But who was he to judge? He regretted the words as he snapped them out, but quickly redeemed them by saying: 'Oh well, we've got that nicely sorted, so subject firmly closed!' He smiled too, but he didn't take her arm as they made their way off the bridge.

As for Charis, she felt a little like a brown paper

parcel again . . . a parcel that he feared might land
in his lap, if he didn't—oh, so quickly—slip it back to
where he hoped it would stay.

'I rang Miss Ivyson this morning to ask how she
was,' she told him. She had to say something, they
couldn't walk on for another five minutes or more in
a prickly silence; it was too uncomfortable.

Guy looked at her sideways, his jacket undone,
hands in his trouser pockets. 'She was all right, was
she?' He moved a stone with his shoe.

'Yes, fine,' said Charis. 'She was at college, I had
to ring her there, but she gave me no message for
Peter Trueman, neither did she say she was going in
to see him. I thought that was rather odd. The other
girl has been in twice—yesterday and today. She even
winkled me out of the sluice and said how sorry she
was for the trouble she'd caused, and she went in to
see Sister too. I would never have known her as the
same *person* . . . butter wouldn't melt! And Peter
was all smiles when he saw her. I couldn't get over it.'

Guy laughed. 'There's no accounting for tastes, nor
for this thing called love. And occasionally, you
know—not always, mind, but just occasionally, an ex-
girl-friend, or ex-flame, whatever you like to call her,
can come back into one's life and fit there, with
gratifying results.'

And you, of course, would know all about that,
Charis could have retorted, but she bit down hard on
her tongue, managing to smile back in pseudo-agree-
ment, and pseudo-amusement, straight into his eyes.
It was astonishing how one's pride could rise to the
top at times like these. Look for look, and thrust for
thrust . . . because hadn't she as good as told him
that she and Neil were still close, or let him think they
were? Not that he cared a toss, of course; whereas
thinking of him with Joanne made an ache inside her
that was nearly anguish. Beautiful, lush Joanne, with

her big eyes and cloud of dark curls misting on to her shoulders.

The sun went in, the breeze freshened. Guy buttoned his jacket. His suits were expensive, the cut perfection; he wore them with an air, yet with carelessness too, a kind of disdain, a haughty elegance, as natural to him as breathing in and out.

'It's going to rain.' Charis looked at the sky.

'It is, and we'd better hurry.'

So they did—they hurried, they practically jogged, and they said goodbye in passing—he to his flat, she to Challoners Lane.

One could almost say they met in passing during the following week, because Athelstone Ward was very busy indeed. Mr Donald Palfrey was discharged home after the weekend. He still had to wear his plastic jacket, and would be attending Outpatients for physio for several weeks to come. But this, he said, didn't worry him. 'I just want to be at home and get three good meals a day, to keep my strength up, Staff!'

Sister told him he had been a good patient, which wasn't strictly true. He knew it too, and winked at Charis. 'My lucky charm got me through. Here it is, look . . . want to see?' He put his hand in his pocket. Out came a piece of blackish fur, as small as a pencil end; it looked hard and stiff.

'What on earth is it?' she wanted to know.

He laughed when she wouldn't touch it. 'It's a mole's foot. I've had it for years, keeps me safe, that does. It's a charm against evil spirits.'

'Which we *don't* have in here!' Sister exclaimed, looking horrified. Robert Peele laughed. He was doing his round; he pulled a face at Charis who, keeping hers straight, got Mr Palfrey and his lucky charm out of the ward, and into the care of his son and daughter-in-law.

His bed was taken by an undergraduate—a Varsity rugger player, with a torn meniscus, a knee injury,

which would require surgery. On the day he was
admitted, Mr Boston was discharged, and on Tuesday
Mr Barry, for Chiari osteotomy, was prepped by
Charis, for surgery at ten. Mr Barry looked older than
his thirty years, he was thin-faced and drawn, his
frown lines made him look anxious, which he insisted
he was not. 'I'm just glad to be in here, glad to be
getting something done,' he said. He had been in the
ward nearly a week, while various tests and procedures
were carried out—not the least of them being to do
with his blood, cross-matching and grouping, haemo-
globin estimation, and a full detailed count. He had
also got to know several other patients; he felt he was
among friends, which wasn't at all a bad feeling
immediately prior to surgery. He watched Charis
cleaning and wiping and dabbing at the skin area over
his pelvis; he felt warmed, sterile towels being applied
and bandaged firmly on. She was quick and deft, she
was smiling and human, which made a world of
difference. Lying on a canvas, with clean sheets, clad
in a hospital gown, he was given his pre-medication
injection of Omnopon and Scopolamine an hour before
he went down to Theatre.

The theatre porters came up to fetch him, but
Charis went with him as well, walking along beside
the trolley, out to the waiting lift. She knew that Sir
Rodney and Guy were operating, assisted by Robert
Peele, backed up, of course, by the nursing team, led
by Joanne Tolbie who would almost certainly be the
instrument nurse. She was in the transfer area when
the trolley was wheeled in. She was standing beyond
the blue line on the sterile side of the bay. In her cap
and mask and theatre gown, she looked anonymous,
apart from her eyes which smiled at Charis over the
top of her mask. This morning she was Theatre Sister
Tolbie, geared and garbed for the job—the important
job of helping two surgeons give a new lease of mobile
life to a man who had never known what it was like

to walk without a caliper, or even to walk without fear of falling down.

He was returned to the ward from the recovery room on a tilting and turning bed, a blood transfusion having taken the place of the original Hartmann's infusion. As well as the customary TPR and blood pressure checks the warmth and colour of his feet and legs had to be observed, in case the blood and nerve supply might have been affected by the operation, or the plaster of Paris itself.

The plaster—the hip spica—was extensive, and as Charis explained to Nurse Adams, half-hourly checks would be necessary over the following twenty-four hours. 'As I'm sure you know, Nurse, the plaster is to keep the hip joint steady. It's been applied from the waist right down to his foot on the bad leg, and to just above the knee on the other side. His legs are held in abduction, to make it easier for us to bed-bath him and see to his toileting. We're going to have to watch pressure areas, in spite of the sheepskin he's lying on. He'll need to be turned at two-hourly intervals.'

'How long will he have to be in the plaster?' Nurse Adams asked, looking down at the soundly sleeping man.

'About a month is usual, after X-rays have confirmed that everything is all right inside it.' Charis moved away from the bed as she saw Sister Holt and Guy Morland, followed by Robert Peéle, coming towards them. She handed Sister the charts. Guy glanced at them, nodded briefly, cast a look at the patient, gave the charts to Charis, then went to the central desk. There, with Sister and Rob beside him, he outlined the care and treatment that Sir Rodney and he wanted the patient to have.

He passed Charis in the corridor a few minutes later. She heard his muttered: 'Good evening, Staff,' but he whisked by at such a speed that by the time she had gathered her wits and replied, he was well out of earshot, pushing his way out of the corridor doors. He had most likely, she thought, come up straight from Theatre, he might even be going back there. He was still in his green gown with his white coat dragged on top. Yet somehow or other, even in that outlandish attire, he still managed to look presentable.

Just before six Charis cycled home, thinking idly about flats, for she knew that very soon she ought to be looking out for one. I must get myself put on an agent's books, she thought. Shall I go through Hansons? Shall I get Neil to handle it for me, or wouldn't he want to help? She didn't see why he wouldn't, it was business, after all—small business, but worthy of the name, and she couldn't see Neil turning it down; he wasn't that kind of man.

How long did it take to get probate through? When would she get her money? Somehow or other she had an idea that those kind of wheels turned slowly . . . very very slowly indeed. She wasn't in any hurry, though, she liked living at Cranleigh. The arrangement she and Nan had devised that lunchtime at the Crown was working well . . . almost *too* well. I shall never want to move, she thought, as she pedalled round to the kitchen door.

Mrs Kent was still there, six o'clock hadn't chimed, and she never left before time. There was a saucepan of home-made soup on the Aga, chops under the grill, vegetables in their saucepans, ready for switching on, a creamy apricot syllabub in the fridge. 'Make a good meal, Miss Littleton,' she said, putting the final touches to a shallow bowl of purple anemones which she placed on the windowsill.

'I can't wait to start it,' said Charis, smiling over at her. Fay Kent didn't look like a housekeeper, more like a hard-working gardener, but then she was that as well, so perhaps the best loved side of her job, and she dearly loved gardening, influenced the rest of her.

She never wore anything but corduroy trousers, with a mannish shirt on top. The sleeves were worn down and the tail was tucked in during the nippy weather; in the summer she had it hanging out and the sleeves rolled up to the elbow; she had cropped yellow-gold hair and bright blue eyes. Her husband, Clive, managed a pet supplies shop on the eastern side of the town. Homer had his meat from there, brought by Mrs Kent in the green estate car she had bought secondhand from Cedric Littleton. She came every day except Sunday, which was the day when she and Clive went birdwatching out in Cowper's Fen.

Charis watched her drive off, then went upstairs to change into dungarees. After supper she decided to do some gardening herself. She felt the need to smell the earth, to get down on her knees and pull out some weeds, and make ready for the seedlings, which Harold would bring next week. Thank goodness Fay Kent wasn't one of those gardeners who went mad if anyone other than themselves dragged up a weed or two. She progressed from the borders to the orchard, right at the top of the garden. Here she raked away rotting leaves and piled them up for compost. She had been right to come out here this evening, she felt worry-free and relaxed; she felt contentment and a kind of inner peace. There were sounds, of course, from other gardens—the whine and whirr of mowers, the occasional slam of a car door, the agitated twittering of a family of blackbirds as they sighted a prowling cat.

Charis began to think about her father, the thoughts becoming so vivid that she felt he was in the garden with her, asking her why in Hades she wanted to give herself all that work when Fay would do it better. One thought, one memory, led to others, and she could see him in his chair up by the rockery, on a summer's morning, reading the *Sunday Express*. She could see him in his oatmeal suit, leaning forward to sniff a rose; see him pensive by the front door, smoking a cigarette through the long silver holder he always used. Regret came then, regret that they hadn't had more time together. She sighed as she experienced a pang of that pointless feeling of 'if only' . . . if only I'd told him just how much I'd loved being here with him. Oh, how she wished he were here now; how she wished she could turn round to see him coming up from the house, telling her to hurry or she'd miss *Panorama* . . . asking where Homer was.

Right at this moment Homer was sitting under the walnut tree, keening, as he spied a bird's nest he couldn't hope to reach. Down in the house the phone was ringing; neither girl nor dog heard it. It rang again an hour later when Charis was in the bath, trying to soak the tiredness from her limbs. She ran down to answer it, wrapped in a dressing-gown, cursing under her breath, feeling more uncomfortably wet than dry. At first she failed to recognise the voice at the other end, then it came in more clearly, much more closely. The caller was Margaret Brodie.

Charis caught her breath. 'Oh, Margaret, he*llo*! Oh, I'm so glad you've rung. Your mother will have told . . . '

'Yes, she has, I'm with her now . . . I'm speaking from Aberdeen. I got back from France two hours ago, I tried to ring you earlier. Charis, I don't know what to say . . . about your father, I mean. I'm so dreadfully sorry . . . I feel so shocked, I just don't know what to say!' Her voice was emotion-charged, and even with five hundred miles between them, Charis felt her sympathy, felt her own throat closing up.

'It was very quick, he wasn't ill long—only a matter of minutes,' she told Margaret. 'Nan and I are glad about that . . . glad he didn't have . . . couldn't have known he was dying, hadn't time to be afraid.' There was no sound from the other end, yet the line was still humming. 'Margaret, are you . . . '

'Yes, I'm still here,' she heard the sound of a cough,

'and I'm afraid there's something I have to ask you. I thought of it at once, when Mother told me what had happened. Charis, did your father before he . . . during his last few days . . . tell Mr Pratt that he'd made a new will, tell him where it was?'

'He most certainly did *not*!' Charis sat down with suddenness on the stairs. She was so surprised that her voice sounded shrill, as though it was tinged with anger—or excitement. 'But what do you mean? Nan and I knew nothing about it. We naturally thought . . . Margaret, what do you mean? When did Father make it?'

'I typed it for him at Hansons just before I left for Scotland, so that would be . . . ' Margaret paused, 'three days before he died. He was adamant that he didn't want to sign it and get it witnessed at the office, so as he was taking me home that night, he came up to the flat and signed it there, and I and my cousin Elspeth witnessed it.'

'But where is it . . . where is it now?'

'Still at my flat,' Margaret replied, hearing, as she did so, the gasp of amazement that Charis gave as she struggled to her feet.

'But . . . why *there* ?'

'Because your father forgot to take it home with him. I found it on my hall table after he'd gone. I rang him, of course, said that Elspeth and I would drop it in at Cranleigh on our way up to Scotland, very early next morning, but he said not to worry, said to leave it where it was, to lock it up for him. I suppose I should have insisted on him having it, but you know how it is . . . I was in a rush to get off, and I'm not good at insisting; I never was, especially where your father was concerned. So I did as he said, I locked it up, I put it in my desk. But he did say he'd see Mr Pratt and tell him what he'd done, and where the will was, and he also said he'd tell you and Mrs Roffey.'

'Well he didn't,' said Charis.

'Which means,' said Margaret, 'that Mr Nigel Pratt will have to cancel what's been done and start all over again. Can you possibly go along to my flat and collect the will tonight? I expect you're on duty early tomorrow?'

'Yes, I am . . . at a quarter to eight.'

'Then go tonight. It's in my desk, at the top, in one of the pigeonholes. Mrs Roffey and you are joint executors, so you'll have to set things in train. If you can't manage to see Pratt tomorrow, ring him and alert him, but get the will to him, and perhaps Mrs Roffey could go along to his office. It's very much in your interests to do so—this new will, which revokes the old one, is favourable to you and your sister.'

'But how will I manage to get into your flat? I can hardly burgle it!' Charis was trying to laugh, but all that came out was a cackling choke; but really, she thought, how *extraordinary* this was! She could hardly believe it.

'You'll need to ring Neil. He can go to Hansons and get my key from there. We're the managing agents for Mayfield Court . . . well, you know that, of course. My key will be there on the board with the rest. So ring him, and ask him to fetch it. He's got his own key to the office, so no problem there. Get him to take you to the flat—don't go on your own. It's getting late and it's dark, and it would be better to have him with you.'

'All right,' Charis said slowly, 'yes, I think that's a good idea. And thank you for ringing so promptly, Margaret. It's very good of you.'

'I'm hardly prompt—not after five weeks,' Margaret sounded upset again. 'I'll be back on Friday, I'll see you then. And, once more, I'm so sorry about it. I thought a lot of your father, and I couldn't even send any flowers.' When she rang off she sounded as though she were crying, or blowing her nose. Charis replaced the phone with a shaking hand.

Margaret had said to ring Neil, but she had no idea, of course, of the new situation—of them being *dis*engaged. Charis sat down on the stairs again, her mind whirling in circles. The person she most wanted to ring was Nan, but she resisted the temptation to reach for the phone and do just that. I mustn't, she thought. I must ring Neil, I must do that first and go to the flat. She began to dial his number. Suppose he was out? He wasn't, he answered the call so quickly that she jumped at the sound of his voice, and exclaimed: 'My goodness, that was quick!'

'I was in the hall, a foot from the phone. It's all right, Mrs Hunt, it's a call for me,' he said in an aside to his plump, bustling landlady who had come out, thinking it might be for her. 'Charis, there's nothing wrong, is there?' His voice came close to her ear.

'Not a thing, quite the reverse.' She told him about the will, and what Margaret had said.

'I'm not surprised, not a bit surprised,' he said in a voice that had strong undertones of, 'I told you so.' There was a pause, as he carefully weighed up what Charis was asking of him. She didn't blame him for hesitating, for even she felt it was slightly off-beat to walk into someone's flat and extract a document from a private desk, at ten o'clock at night. Even with permission, even with a key, there was something sleuthy about it; it wouldn't seem quite so bad if it were light. 'Okay, will do,' Neil said at last. 'I'll go to the office first, get the key, then come round for you in fifteen minutes' time.'

'Neil, you *are* sure? I mean, I don't want . . .'

'Of course I'm sure,' he said. 'The sooner this thing's cleared up the better. Margaret's perfectly right.' He rang off then, and Charis got dressed, warmly and sensibly, in a velour leisure suit and loafers, her hair tied back in a pony tail. She was ready and waiting on the front steps when Neil turned into the lane, dipping his lights as he backed the car into the drive.

'It's good of you to turn out like this, Neil. I didn't like asking you,' she said, sliding in beside him and turning to look at him, 'but Margaret made such an issue of getting the will tonight, and I have to admit that—well, that I'm dying to know what it says.'

'You wouldn't,' said Neil, watching her as she fastened her safety belt, 'be human if you didn't feel that way, and I'm glad to be involved. As to its being good of me—well, what are friends for?'

'Thank you, I hoped you'd say that,' she smiled. He let in the clutch and the car moved smoothly down the lane to the first set of traffic lights. Charis sat back, still feeling bemused. It was like some sort of dream.

'I assume you didn't tell Margaret Brodie that you'd jilted me,' said Neil.

'No, of course I didn't!'

'Why, of course?'

'Well, there wasn't . . . I didn't . . . have time. Besides, it wasn't like that, was it? We simply agreed not to marry.'

'I can't go along with that entirely, but still, never mind,' he said. The lights were red, he braked and stopped, turned and glanced at her. It seemed entirely natural to him to have her in the car. He had never wanted to break the engagement, he hadn't been trying to end it when he suggested they postponed things for a while. He had been nervous about going ahead too fast without her father behind them. His sudden death, not getting the partnership, had shaken him to the core. Charis not getting the inheritance she deserved had been a bitter blow. With money behind them he could have broken from Hansons, made a completely new start, opened his own office—yes, that had been in his mind. He would never have taken a penny from Charis without paying proper interest. *That* side would have been business; the other side would have worked out . . . with her it would have worked out, and if she wouldn't have him, he knew he would never marry anyone else.

CHAPTER NINE

THEY turned into College Walk, when after another half-mile or so, Mayfield Court could be seen amongst the trees. 'Well, here we are,' Neil said prosaically, pulling into the forecourt. He spoke quietly, in just above a whisper—it was that kind of situation. Charis found herself doing exactly the same.

Rows of windows looked down at them, some were lit and some were not. Guy's were in darkness, Charis saw, flicking a glance upwards. Good, she thought; that meant he was out. While engaged on this sort of errand, the last thing she wanted was to run into him. All she wanted was to get in and out of the flat with lightning speed, and back home, and on the phone to Nan.

They walked up the first flight of stairs to the landing, and there was Margaret's front door, with a large white 'No.8' over the letterbox. Neil unlocked it and stepped inside first, Charis following. He felt for and switched on the light. 'We don't have to snoop,' he said. He made to open the wrong inner door, but Charis tugged at his arm.

'I rather think,' she told him, moving to the right, 'that this is the door to the sitting-room.' He opened it, and it was. Margaret's flat had the same layout as Guy Morland's above it. Her carpet was darker than his, while her furniture was chintzy. An oil painting of a mare and her foal hung over the fireplace, a bureau-type desk stood in the window bay.

'Well, there it is.' Neil moved towards it. 'Do you want to look, or shall I?' He stood with one hand on its walnut slope, but already he was pulling at each of the drawers, and at the top—the part that should have let down, and showed pigeonholes and another drawer, perhaps. Nothing budged a quarter-inch. 'It's locked! Didn't Margaret say?'

Charis shook her head; she couldn't speak. He tried the drawers again. 'Unless she's got the keys in her handbag, up in Scotland,' he said, 'they *have* to be somewhere here in the flat.'

'We can't search it . . . it wouldn't be right.' Charis found her voice at last. Why on earth hadn't she thought to ask Margaret whether the desk would be locked and, if so, where she would find the key? She looked helplessly at Neil, and he at her, then he slammed a hand to his head.

'Charis, I'll ring her . . . I'll ring her up! I've got her number with me, here in my diary,' he pulled it out of his pocket and turned to the back. 'Yes, here it is—I had it, you remember, when we tried to get in touch when your father died. If the keys are here, she'll tell us where to look.'

'Yes, all right . . . yes, do that.' She watched him pick up the phone. It seemed like hours as she stood there waiting . . . waiting for him to get through. In fact it was minutes only, and Margaret was quick to tell him that they would find the keys on a nail behind the painting over the fireplace.

'I'd completely forgotten I hadn't told Charis. I'll hang on,' she said, 'till you've got the desk open and found the will, then I'll know my part is done. It's at the top, in one of the pigeonholes.'

'Good . . . thanks.' Neil laid the receiver on the arm of one of the chairs, then went to the painting, found the keys, unlocked the top of the desk. There were six pigeonholes, all crammed with papers; he helped Charis search. They were both standing in front of the desk, sifting and sorting through it, when they heard the sound of the sitting-room door grazing

over the carpet, and turning round, they saw Guy
Morland and Joanne Tolbie staring at them. Guy's
face was tight with suspicion, Joanne's wide with
surprise.

'May I ask what you're doing here?' Guy enquired.

'We're on legitimate business,' Neil told him, turning
back to the desk, turning his back on Guy too. Charis
quickly explained.

'We've got Margaret's permission to be here. She
asked us to come . . . to find a document . . . as
a matter of fact, it's my father's will. Margaret had it
locked up here, and none of us knew about it, until
tonight, when she rang me at home.' Her voice petered
out. She felt embarrassed and, quite unjustly, *guilty,*
as she stood there in front of Guy and Joanne,
explaining her piece.

Neil was carrying on with the search. He appeared
to have opted out of any attempt to try to explain
their presence in the flat. The truth was he saw no
need to explain, he was in the right and he knew it.
He didn't like Morland, he never had. Who does he
think he is? he thought, as he straightened up with the
will in his hand.

'Here it is, darling.' He gave it to Charis, whose
fingers closed over the envelope, clearly marked, 'Last
Will & Testament of Cedric Henry Littleton.' She
made to show it to Guy, then abruptly changing her
mind, tucked it into her handbag and closed the zip.

'Check up on us if you want to,' she said. 'Margaret
is on the phone . . . hanging on, over there,' she
pointed to the receiver, lying limp and mute on the
arm of the chintzy chair.

They measured glances. He trusted her, surely . . .
he knew her well enough to be certain she wouldn't
have come here in a snooping capacity. If he speaks
to Margaret and asks her to corroborate what I've
said, I'll never feel the same about him . . . I'll never
forgive him for that, she thought. She was willing him

not to go to the phone, she *wanted* him to trust her, but already he was moving towards it, picking it up and speaking.

'Is that Miss Brodie? Guy Morland here . . . yes, I'm in your flat. I saw the door ajar and lights on, so I came to investigate. I understand that . . . ' He stopped speaking then, as Margaret was filling him in. At the end of it all Charis heard him say, 'That's all right . . . only too glad. Goodbye, yes, safe journey home.' He handed the phone to Neil, who practically snatched it from his hand. Assuring Margaret that they had found the will and were on the point of leaving, he replaced the receiver. 'I should imagine,' he said, locking the desk with a flourish, 'that Miss Brodie will have a telephone bill the length of my hand and arm.

'From Land's End to John O'Groats!' Joanne put in smartly, standing there in her blue dress of clinging crêpe-de-chine, a lacy shawl hanging over one arm. She was showing a good deal of cleavage, Charis noticed, looking away from her, and meeting, as she did so, Guy's studied stare.

'I'm sorry I delayed things even further,' he said in chilly tones, 'but if you'd taken the trouble to close the flat door, I wouldn't have been alerted.'

'Oh, Guy darling, the drama's over, let's get back to where we belong . . . *all* of us.' Joanne smiled at Charis, tugging Guy to the door. 'You know, there are times when I wonder if you ought to have been a policeman. I can recognise one or two very policeman-like traits!'

During the short journey home in the car Charis concentrated solely on the document in her handbag, because that was all that mattered. She refused to dwell on the scene in the flat, and when Neil remarked rather crossly: 'That man has very inflated ideas of his own importance, you know,' she didn't spring to Guy's defence, just said how sorry she was about the whole thing, and thanked him for helping her.

She assumed that he would drive off, once he had dropped her at Cranleigh, but no, he got out when she did, and made his way to the steps, just as he had always done when they were engaged. So she had to ask him in after that . . . she couldn't brush him off, not after all he had done for her tonight.

His welcome from Homer was unstinted. The dog licked his face all over, paws up on his shoulders, eyes soft with love. 'Take him back and marry him,' Homer seemed to be saying, 'take him back and let's have a man in the house.'

'I'll wait in the sitting-room while you talk to Nan.' Neil grasped Homer's collar.

'Okay, yes . . . switch the fire on.' Charis took the will from her bag. The envelope was sealed, but bore the names of the two executors—Nan and herself—which surely meant it was all right to open it. She dialled the Roffeys' number, and stood there holding her breath. Seconds later she was reading the document over to her sister, who had shrieked at her to: '*Open* it . . . let's hear what it's all about!'

She very soon knew; they both did. Cranleigh House and contents were left to Charis, and so were some shares, the income from which would be sufficient to keep it running and pay Mrs Kent. She had also been left a painting by Holdstein, at present at the bank. Nan's inheritance was greater in value. 'Owing to the fact that she is my elder daughter,' Cedric had said in the will. It came to Nan in the form of gilt-edged securities. She was also left her own mother's antique furniture. Mrs Kent had the sum of a thousand pounds, and Helen Jean Keldos, Charis's maternal grandmother, had a parcel of oil shares. The residue of the estate would go to charity. Both Charis and Nan thought justice had been done.

Nan was cock-a-hoop with delight. 'Good old Dad!' she cried. 'Oh, Charis, isn't it marvellous, marvellous!

He *didn't* let us down! Hold on while I just tell Harold! Oh, it's exactly what I wanted!' she carolled, as though she had just been given a present from under the Christmas tree. Charis could hear her shouting for Harold to come.

They drove over from Little Molding. The late hour didn't matter; they had to be together, they had to talk about it. Just after midnight, Nan and Harold and Charis and Neil drank a toast to the memory of Cedric Littleton: 'To Dad, God bless him!' Nan raised her glass. Charis silently echoed that, recalling as she did so the thoughts she had had that evening in the garden, when her father had seemed so close.

Nan announced that she would take the will, telephone Mr Pratt, and go to see him as soon as he could fit her in next morning. 'I suppose it *will* be all right,' she said. 'He'll be able to cancel the arrangements made in connection with the other will?' She was looking straight at Harold, but in the end it was Neil who answered her.

'There'll be no difficulty, none, but of course the sooner he knows the better. As a matter of fact the question of wills came up the other day, when I visited Peter Trueman in hospital up in Charis's ward. I can't remember how we got on the subject but he quoted an instance where a valid will had been found, revoking a former one. Corrective forms were made out and all was well.'

'That's good.' Nan finished her sherry. Harold touched Charis's hand. 'You're quiet, love,' he remarked.

'I'm a little tired. I'm not quiet because I'm not pleased. I *am* pleased, for all sorts of reasons. I love this house, you know, and now I'll be able to stay here for always, if I choose.'

'Yes, you will, and I'm glad for you.' Harold's eyes remained on her face. To his way of thinking Charis looked far too grave for her twenty-four years. His gaze moved to Neil. Was he the cause? Would they mend their breach? He didn't dare ask, but Nan, made extra loquacious by two sherries, appeared to have abandoned every qualm.

'The best thing you two can do is get married, and live here,' she said. 'It was all nonsense, breaking up as you did.' She pushed herself to her feet. 'Come on, Harold, we ought to be going. I'll ring you tomorrow, Charis. It's a good job I'm not driving, isn't it . . . good job Harold's teetotal!' They were off and away down the lane in minutes. 'Those two ought to get married,' Nan said again, but Harold didn't reply.

Neil decided he would walk home and pick up the car in the morning. He didn't want to get breathalysed, he said. He went off with considerable awkwardness. He didn't quite know how to get himself out of the house, nor what to say as he did so. 'I'm very pleased,' he said haltingly, 'about the will, I mean. I know you think—oh, never mind, I'd better just take myself off. Let me know if I can help again, in any way at all. As I said earlier, what are friends for if they can't jump to it and turn to one another in times of need?'

'Thanks, Neil.' She saw him out, and he walked down the steps past his car, down to the gates, where he turned and called out 'Goodbye' once again, before she went in and closed the door.

Charis slept in fits and starts that night, dreaming partly of Athelstone Ward . . . in her dream, though, it was a baby ward, with rows of incubators instead of a line of plastered arms and legs. And waking at five a.m. brought the last night's happenings flooding back. The house was hers, or it would be soon. It was hers to do what she liked with. It gave her a heady feeling of independence to realise that. It helped to mitigate other feelings that stuck like pins in her mind—Guy thinking she had gone with Neil to Margaret's flat on a pillaging trip, not believing her explanation, checking up on her. Another insidious pinprick was the remembered sight of Joanne walking with him up to his flat, as though she lived there with him. Well, perhaps she does, and if she does, it's no business of mine, Charis told herself sternly, drawing back the curtains on a rainy morning and a cloud-hung lowering sky.

The rest of the week passed swiftly, with Margaret returning from Scotland at the weekend, and coming to visit her. By then Nigel Pratt, having satisfied himself that the new will was in order, had prepared and sent off another set of forms. Charis asked Margaret if there was anything of her father's she would like to have, to which she replied that she already had something she prized very much—the painting of the horses that Charis had seen in her flat. 'He gave it to me twelve years ago, he picked it up at a sale, together with the Holdstein that's been left to you,' she said without thanking her. 'I had mine valued for insurance purposes only just recently, suffi-cient to say that if I needed to sell it, it would keep me for several years . . . not that I want to, but one has to be practical. Now that your father has died I don't feel I want to stay at Hansons. Neil and I match one another in unsettlement just at the moment, *and* in unhappiness. I'm sorry you had to treat him as you did.' Her tone was blaming, her eyes accusing. Charis blinked in amazement. This was a side to Margaret Brodie she had never seen before.

'It wasn't like that, Margaret,' she said, but she didn't go on to explain. She was thankful when Margaret got up to go.

At the end of the following week Sister Holt went on leave, and Guy, whom Charis had only seen in the company of others for the past ten days, came to do his round. He made his way to the office first to tell her about a patient who was being admitted on Sunday, the following day. 'He's a sixty-four-year-old aircraft engineer, name of Bernard Maxwell. He suffers from peripheral vascular disease, and Sir Rodney and I agree that a mid-thigh amputation of his right leg is vital. I've got to know him through his Outpatients' visits. He's conditioned to losing his leg, tells me he's had worse fears than that, and says he can cope. I hope to operate on Thursday and in the time up until then he may as well see Mrs Dixon and the occupational therapist, also Harvey, the limb fitter . . . get to know them all.'

'Yes, of course, I'll arrange it.' Charis made a note on her pad. As she did so she was aware of Guy standing in front of the desk, so close that the front of his starched white coat rasped the edges of it. As she raised her head she surprised him looking down at her. He glanced away quickly, turning to the door.

'I don't want to do a full round,' he said. 'This is my weekend off, but now that I'm here I may as well see the meniscectomy patient and Peter Trueman . . . oh yes, and Giles Barry, I think.'

'I've got their notes here, I was just going through them.' Charis got up with the folders. She expected him to open the door and go out, but he made no move to do so.

'Are you well?' he enquired.

'Yes, perfectly well.' Why the concern? she wondered, unaware that since her father's death her face was paler and thinner. The fragile graveness that Harold had noticed only the other evening wasn't lost on Guy who, after all, was trained to observe such things. 'Why do you ask?' Her tone was cool, she deliberately made it so.

'Because you're going to need to be in top form for the next fortnight, aren't you? We don't want you falling down on the job.'

'That won't be the case,' she assured him.

'I'm glad to hear it. So what do I call you . . . Staff or Acting Sister?' His mouth curved in the kind of smile she didn't like very much.

'I'm sticking to Staff,' she said bluntly. 'People know me as that, anyway.' She eased round the desk and walked towards him. He opened the door at once.

'Right then, Staff, let's get on, shall we?' He let her go out first, then brushed past her into the ward so quickly that in his haste he knocked the folders of notes from under her arm. Even then he didn't stop, just flung out a 'Sorry' over his shoulder, while she bent to pick them up.

'The age of chivalry's dead, Staff.' Molly Silver, the domestic, said, coming in with her tray of mid-morning drinks. 'He's a lovely-looking man, mind, but what I always say is, handsome is as handsome does.'

'Mr Morland's in a hurry,' Charis said, defending him and going to Peter Trueman's bed, where Guy stood containing his impatience till the notes were put in his hand. Peter Trueman, after six weeks in bed, was getting very fed up. Mrs Dixon, the physiotherapist, had taught him movements of his knee, plus active exercises of his toes, foot and ankle. Even so, he wanted to know when he could start weight-bearing.

'We'll try you with a walking frame in three or four weeks' time,' Guy told him, 'as by then your arm should be out of plaster.'

'Trust me to bust up both limbs!'

'Yes, well, it's been known before.'

'I'm anxious to get home . . . extra anxious. I'm getting married this summer. Claire and I want to set a date.'

'By the end of June you'll be fit for most things,' Guy commented drily, raising his brows a fraction as he and Charis moved away. 'It seems the fair Melissa has lost the battle, Staff.'

'I don't think she entered it. She just left the way clear for the other more forceful type.'

'Well, I'm glad they didn't take up cudgels here in

the ward again.' His eyes moved to the clock on the
wall, then to the view from the windows—a view of
cloudless azure sky, and warm May sunshine; he could
feel its rays striking the back of his neck.

Dick Rosen, the varsity rugger player, was the star
of the ward, or the ward jester; he kept his neighbours
amused. He was good at imitations, both of the
nursing and medical staff. He was a short young man
with wide shoulders, a ruddy healthy complexion,
good sound teeth and a ready smile. It was amazing
how he could contort his features and reconstruct his
voice to look and sound like Sir Rodney Barks, or
Rob, or Guy Morland, or even the diminutive Sister
Holt. He had had his operation—the excision of a
torn meniscus—six days ago, and was making good
progress, but Guy had decided that he must remain
in hospital until his sutures were removed. He was
having intensive physiotherapy to give tone to his
quadriceps muscle; stiffness and pain were decreasing
every day. He asked the same question as most healthy
young adults who couldn't wait to be active again:
'When am I likely to be discharged?'

Guy picked up a copy of *Rugby World* from the
top of his locker, looked at the cover, put it down
again, then answered his questions. 'As soon as you
can raise that leg of yours straight in the air, you'll
get a pair of crutches by way of reward. Then once
you've mastered those, once you can walk with just a
stick, I'll probably consider you fit for discharge.'

''Course there'll be some things I'll miss,' Dick
Rosen said, openly ogling Charis. He adored her cute
little turned-up nose, that gorgeous curvy mouth, and
he'd always been a push-over for thick, glossy hair,
the colour of honey from the comb. He wondered
what she would say if he asked her for a date. Turn
him down flat, most likely, he decided, watching her
and Guy Morland make their way to bed number
twelve.

Giles Barry, the patient in the hip spica, now eleven days post-op, had Mrs Dixon, the physio, with him; the curtains were drawn round his bed. She was teaching him how to exercise his arms, to strengthen the muscles enough to enable him to use crutches once he was out of his spica. The occupational therapist had provided a beanbag pillow for extra support. She had also laid a pair of tongs called a 'helping hand' on his bed. These were to enable him to reach things more easily from his lying-down position. He had been upset not to be able to do more for himself. He longed to be able to sit up, which, of course, was impossible. 'I feel like a snared rabbit,' he complained, when Mrs Dixon had gone. 'Is everything going as it should, do you think?'

Guy pulled up a chair and sat down. He could see he couldn't hurry this one, and he didn't intend to try. 'You're doing splendidly,' he told Giles Barry, 'exactly as we hoped. In another twelve to fourteen days we'll get an X-ray taken. If that shows the result we expect, we'll be able to take off your plaster. After that you'll be able to sit up, and be gradually mobilised. There'll be difficulty in walking at first, but that will ease with time.'

'So long as there's nothing going wrong, Mr Morland.'

'I promise you there's not. Why, you may be back teaching again in time for the end of term! You'll certainly be there for the start of the autumn term in September. Just bear with us for a little while longer. We're not such a bad lot, you know.'

And when he smiles like that, Charis thought, how could anyone fail to find new strengths to draw on? He's a very remarkable man. How I wish . . . but at that point she slammed down hard on her thoughts. It was no good wishing for miracles. Miracles didn't happen, not in real life, they only cropped up in books.

Rob arrived to complete the round, and Guy went off. In the office later, over coffee, Rob told Charis that G.M. was off to the south coast. 'He told me so yesterday. I bet it's Brighton,' he grinned, as he snapped a ginger biscuit in two. 'Looks like our Joanne's going with him. She was sitting in his car when I crossed the yard, looking creamy about the gills. She means everyone to know about their liaison, doesn't she? She flaunts him like some sort of flag. You wouldn't call her reticent!'

'I suppose we all show off at times,' Charis said, stirring her coffee, then pushing it on to one side, she asked Rob to sign the prescriptions. Collecting the basket, she went down to Pharmacy.

CHAPTER TEN

BERNARD Maxwell was admitted on Sunday morning—a tall, slightly stooping man, with thick brown hair and wide-spaced intelligent eyes. He wasn't a man to be fooled, Charis thought, when after his wife had gone she helped him to settle down into the ward. He was a sensible type yet, paradoxically, he was also superstitious. She discovered this when listing his possessions for locking away in the safe. He refused to allow the St Christopher charm which he wore round his neck on a chain to be taken from him. 'It's my talisman, the keeper of my safety,' he told her smilingly. 'It was given to me during the war when I went into the RAF. It looked after me then, it's done so since; it will keep on doing so now. It gives me courage,' he added simply. So what could Charis say?

Well, at least, she thought, as she left his bed, at least it's not a mole's foot! Yet in a way she wished it was, for the little St Christopher, and the chain he hung from, looked liked solid gold. Would Sister Holt have been firmer about it being locked up? Most likely she would. Charis stood at he desk, arguing with herself. It would have to be taken off him when he went to theatre, but that was days away yet; there seemed no point in upsetting him at this early stage when he needed reassurance from every source. I've done the right thing, she decided, leaving the ward.

During the next four days Mr Maxwell had a highly nutritious diet, supplemented with both oral and intra-muscular vitamins. He was visited by Mrs Dixon, who taught him breathing exercises; the limb-fitter showed

him the type of false leg he would have. Bernard was
intrigued with the hinged knee, and jokingly
commented that at least he wouldn't get arthritis in it.
'All I need to do is oil it, if I hear it creak!' he laughed.
Either Guy or Rob saw him every day, and he had
visitors in plenty. His wife and sister always came, so
did his stepdaughter Lucy, looking bored and sulky,
constantly chewing gum. She was fifteen and her
mother insisted on the visits. She was desperately
trying to improve the relationship between her husband
and her daughter. Bernard was her second husband;
she had divorced Lucy's father two years ago, and she
sometimes felt that the girl had never forgiven her,
nor forgiven Bernard, who was just about the kindest,
most gentle man who ever lived. Lucy *must* get to love
him in time.

He was far more reasonable that Charis had antic-
ipated about parting with the St Christopher on the
morning she got him ready for theatre. But he still
wouldn't let her lock it away in Sister's safe. 'No, I
want it kept here in my locker, amongst all my things.
Put it in that brown purse, then when I'm back here
in bed, you can take it out and fasten it round my
neck.'

'Mr Maxwell, you'll still be very dozy, you'll scarcely
know what's happening.' But all the nurses are trus-
tworthy, so what am I worrying about? Why am I
making such a fuss? Charis asked herself.

'Are you saying that someone might nick it?'
Although his eyes were brown, they nevertheless had
a look of Guy Morland's, especially when he frowned.

'I just want you to realise that we, the Hospital,
can't be held responsible for any lost valuables, unless
you hand them over.'

'Spare me the small print!' There was no mistaking
the steel in his gaze.

'All right, Mr Maxwell, I'll do as you say. The
minute you're back in bed, I'll reunite you with your

charm; I'll see that it's round your neck. But it's us who'll get you well, you know, not a gold St Christopher.'

He relaxed after that, and joked as Charis got him into a hospital gown. 'It's a bit like a choirboy's surplice,' he laughed as she fastened the tapes at the neck. He had a white cap over his hair and a stocking on his good leg. 'There's not an awful lot of point in keeping the other one warm, not for such a short time.' He looked at his right leg for the last time before Charis covered him up. Soon after that he had his pre-med, and just before ten Charis went with him down to Theatre Block.

Sister Tolbie was on leave, so Rob told Charis when he came to do his round. 'She'll be off for a week—she's gone to London; she told me yesterday. Staff Nurse Garde is standing in for her, so she'll be waiting on Guy. They all fall over themselves to do his bidding, you know.'

'Which is probably why he's so autocratic,' Charis said quietly. Rob grimaced and led the way into the ward.

After he had finished the round Charis, watched by Nurse Adams, removed the sutures from young Dick Rosen's knee. He had achieved straight leg raising two days ago. He had been measured for crutches, and there they were, leaning against the wall. In a little while Mrs Dixon and Charis were going to get him walking. He was excited, but nervous. 'You've no need to worry,' Charis assured him. 'With all the exercises you've been having in bed, your muscles are toned and strong. You'll soon be walking round the ward, getting in everyone's way!'

'You're my favourite nurse, do you know that?' He took her hand and kissed it.

'Now I'm sure you say that to all the girls. You've got a good line in patter!' she told him, laughing, as she wheeled the trolley away.

Bernard Maxwell came back from Theatre towards the end of visiting time. He was received into a warmed bed, with fracture boards under the mattress; sandbags were placed on either side of his stump to hold it steady. A bed cradle went over the top, and the bedclothes were enveloped so that the limb could be seen from the foot of the bed. He was woozy and disorientated, but keeping to her promise, Charis fastened the little St Christopher round his neck.

Guy came up to the ward as the visitors had gone. He went straight to Bernard Maxwell, glanced at his charts, nodded as though satisfied. Then he spent a few moments watching Dick Rosen manipulating his crutches. Getting up from the chair and down again was proving difficult. 'Take-off and landing are often hazardous,' said Guy, praising him. 'What we're after is a four-point walk yes,—that's the way . . . you've got it. Right crutch forward, left foot forward . . . left crutch forward, right foot forward, like a quadruped; have you got any pain in your knee?'

'A little, not much, it's stiff more than anything.'

'Try again tomorrow,' advised Guy, as Dick flopped back on his chair.

Charis went off duty at four-thirty, leaving Peggy Barford in charge. Most of the ambulant patients were up then, looking forward to an evening of television, or chess, or Scrabble; and then shortly before supper there would be visiting again, just for half an hour.

Guy Morland was coming out of Docherty Ward as Charis crossed the landing. The lift was crowded, but they managed to squeeze themselves in. Facing him, standing jammed against him, caused a slide of sensations in Charis. Yet somehow she managed to school her face to hide how her body betrayed her by its weakness . . . yes, its weakness . . . where this stern-eyed man was concerned.

As soon as the lift touched ground, as soon as the metal doors slid back, she was across the entrance hall in seconds, only to pull up short as she saw coming in from the tarmac yard a woman with two large cases . . . a small, dainty woman in a grey flannel suit. She stared and heard herself gasp. Surely it couldn't be . . . surely it wasn't . . . but it was, it was, it was! It was her grandmother, it was Helen from Greece, all the way from Athens . . . it was Helen! She ran into her grandmother's arms. 'Helen, I can't *believe* it!'

Helen Keldos held her close. 'I decided to spring a surprise. Maybe I should have let you know, but in the end I just came. I left Athens at ten this morning, I'm over here for a month. If you can't put me up . . .'

'Can't put you up? Helen, you have to be joking! I've got a whole house to do it in—three bedrooms going spare.' As they bent to pick up the cases Guy caught up with them. He had watched their enthusiastic greeting of one another with interest.

'May I help with that luggage?' he enquired.

'We're going out with it, not coming in,' Helen Keldos smiled. Charis introduced them, and saw the look they exchanged. So this, Guy thought, is the grandmother who married a Greek doctor and who nursed at St Mildred's, London Bridge. He remembered Charis mentioning her at the Stantons' party in February. It struck him that forty years on from now Charis would look very much like her—very much like this Mrs Keldos with her pert little nose, her fading gold hair drawn back in a chignon, all-seeing green-hazel eyes, neat bud figure clothed in the grey flannel suit.

'I'll drive you home,' he said to Charis. 'You can hardly transport Mrs Keldos on your bicycle, not with her cases as well.'

'We can get a taxi.'

'You have one,' he replied, as he picked up the

cases. Brooking no further argument, he led the way into the yard.

'I came here first because I didn't know if there would be anyone at Cranleigh,' said Helen as she slid into the front seat of Guy's cream Audi, reaching for and fastening her safety belt.

'Suppose I hadn't been on duty?' Charis asked, from the rear.

'My vibes told me you were,' she said. They laughed, and Charis reflected that she had probably inherited her vibes from Helen, and it was then with a shaft of anxiety that she thought of Bernard Maxwell and the gold St Christopher charm. But why should this trouble her? What could go wrong? No one was going to harm him, or steal the charm. She was being ridiculous.

Helen stared out at the Seftonbridge scene—at the grandeur of Princes Parade, at the huge-candled chestnut tree by the University Library, at St Saviour's lawns, and the low white Senate House. 'It's so lovely to be in England again,' she remarked to Guy Morland, as he carried her cases into Cranleigh a few minutes later.

'Thank you for helping us,' said Charis, trying to make herself heard above Homer's barking and Mrs Kent's surprised cries of greeting. Fay Kent always looked forward to Helen's annual visits. 'Stay for a drink,' Charis mouthed, but Guy smiled and shook his head.

'No, I won't butt in just now. You'll have a lot to talk about. Enjoy your holiday, Mrs Keldos,' he called above the din. He was gone before Charis could see him to the door.

'What a charming man,' observed Helen, as they settled themselves in the sitting-room for a quick drink while Mrs Kent bustled about upstairs. 'I thought by what you said in your letters that he was one of those caustic types, or do I mean 'sarcastic', but he isn't, not a bit.'

'He has many good points—he's a wonderful surgeon, he cares about his patients,' Charis told her.

'I could do with someone like him at the clinic,' Helen said thoughtfully. The Vitura Clinic had a long waiting list, and she wanted to add a new wing. She was always on the look-out for staff, and had several British nurses. 'I could do with someone like you out there too. Now that your father has gone . . . ' she said this quickly—hardened nurse or no, Cedric's death had hurt her—'now that your father's gone and you've split up with Neil, I did just wonder if you might consider it. Oh, not now, darling . . . it's just like me to plunge in too quickly. Five minutes in the house and I'm trying to recruit you! Forget it for the time being.' Mrs Kent came in to announce that her bedroom was ready, and she went upstairs, leaving Charis to her thoughts.

When she went on duty next morning she was met by Night Sister Lomas, who told her that Bernard Maxwell's condition was giving cause for concern. 'He's been asking for his St Christopher. I expect you've got it locked up. I looked in the obvious place, in the safe, but couldn't see it there. I think you ought to let him have it, he's plainly one of those patients who think that a charm on a chain works flaming miracles!' Sister Lomas rarely swore, but she always did so when worried. Bernard Maxwell's systolic blood pressure reading ten minutes ago had been under ninety mm Hg. She had sent for Guy Morland. She was very uneasy, so much so that she failed to notice the look of blanched horror on Staff Nurse Littleton's face.

'But, Sister,' Charis choked out the words, 'I put the St Christopher charm round his neck yesterday afternoon about half past four! I put it on as soon as he came up from the recovery room. He'd made me promise to do that when I prepped him for Theatre.'

'That's a stupid thing to do, Staff. It should have been locked up, and kept there till he was fully conscious . . . you must have been out of your mind!'

'It must have come off, slipped into his bed, inside his gown.'

The rest of the shift came into the office and Sister gave the report. As soon as she had gone off duty, Charis hurried into the ward. Nurse Varden was sitting with Bernard Maxwell. He was pale, with a cold clammy skin, his breathing was shallow and rapid; he saw Charis and moved his hand, and she bent down low to catch his words: 'Didn't . . . do what . . . I asked.'

Disturbing him as little as possible, she felt inside his gown. His bed was due to be made, so she and Nurse Varden stripped off the clothes. There was no sign of the little St Christopher. She daren't tell him it was missing, it was best to let him think it was in safe keeping for the time being.

'We'll get it for you soon,' she told him, just as Guy Morland arrived at the bedside. The cuff of the blood pressure reading machine was in place on Bernard Maxwell's arm. Guy tightened it, and took a reading, his expression deadpan.

'You'll be feeling better presently,' he said to Mr Maxwell, then he moved away with Charis to the desk. 'Set up a drip,' he gave her the details, 'thirty drops per minute. He seems to be distressing himself about that charm of his. Better let him have it. Absurd though it sounds, lucky charms have their place at times. They set the mind at rest for some people, and we none of us know what strange effect the working of the mind has on our physical state.'

'But it's missing,' Charis said thickly. She went on to explain.

'Great Scott!' His face darkened.

'We've looked all over the place . . . everywhere we can think of . . . in his bed, inside his gown. He was adamant that he wanted it on him when he came from Theatre. I couldn't . . . not . . . do as he said,' her voice trailed off. Guy wasn't agreeing with her, she could tell that from his face.

'Well, you'd better tell the SNO and question your nurses.' He went off looking clipped and angry. Charis felt sure he blamed her. Oh, how she wished Sister Holt was there . . . please, Mr Maxwell, get better! She prayed. She picked up the phone and dialled Miss Jay's number with shaking fingers. She told her what had occurred.

It was the longest day she had ever known. Miss Jay, the SNO, came up to the ward. She questioned Charis and the other nurses, and was back in the office in the afternoon when Mrs Maxwell came to visit her husband. His condition and the loss of the charm were explained to her.

'But when Lucy and I came in last night they said he was doing fine; they said he was going to be okay, gave us no warning of this.' She looked frightened, even accusing; her small pinched face was white.

'Did you notice if he was wearing the St Christopher then?' asked Charis. Guy was standing by Mrs Maxwell, and she felt him glance her way.

'No, I didn't. I'm so used to it being round his neck that I don't really see it any more, it's like a part of *him*. And I wasn't thinking about it, was I? But I know what faith he puts in it. It got him and his crew through three operational tours in the war. That's when it all started, he's convinced it keeps him safe. Does he know it's missing, that it might have been stolen?' she looked Charis full in the face.

'Staff has told him it's missing, she couldn't help it in the end,' said Guy; then disregarding the last part of her outburst, he took her arm and led her into the ward.

Bernard Maxwell was febrile and restless, he didn't
know his wife. His infusion had had to be discon-
tinued as, two hours ago, a small thrombosis had
occurred at the needle site. Nurse Varden was with
him, he was never left, the curtains were drawn round
his bed.

Meantime, Miss Jay, Guy Morland and Charis
conferred in the office. 'I shall go to the Nurses' Home
at five,' Miss Jay said. 'The two first-year nurses who
were on duty last night may remember something that
will help.'

'Both Night Sister and I had a word with them this
morning, but they didn't come up with anything, just
said they'd not seen the charm,' said Charis, holding
on to the desk.

'Even so, I'll talk to them.' Miss Jay pursed her
lips. She went out, leaving Charis and Guy alone.

'It's all my fault,' Charis said hopelessly, 'I should
never have put on the charm until he was fully
conscious. Night Sister Lomas was right.'

Guy shook his head. 'I don't agree. You did what
you were asked. Maxwell's condition—whether
brought on by stress, or reaction to surgery—is no
fault of yours, so set your mind at rest.' His words
were emphatic, and to Charis's surprise she felt him
touch her cheek in a light caress before he left the
room.

And perhaps his belief in her, his confidence in her,
the way he had allied with her, made her thinking
clearer, her mind more alert and receptive to possibil-
ities. Mrs Maxwell hadn't taken the charm, but what
about the daughter—Bernard Maxwell's stepdaughter
who never seemed to want to be in the ward, and who
chewed all the time, and never bothered to talk?
Would she have had the opportunity to take the charm
from his neck? Charis thought not. So what was
left . . . *who* was left? One of the nurses, or patient-
s—one of the walking patients? Never, *never* . . .

she didn't believe it. So where had it gone? Where had it gone? It was then that she had an idea. She remembered something that one of the young night nurses had said: 'I had to change his gown in the night, and his neck was as bare as mine.' Change his gown . . . change his gown . . . she had had to change his gown. She had probably changed it in a hurry, changed it in a dim light; she could have been wearing disposable gloves, she might not have noticed if a fine gold chain had got tangled up with the tapes at the back of his neck. And in that case . . . in that case . . . Charis's excitement rose . . . in that case the charm could have been bundled and rolled up in the gown. Right now, at this moment, it could be in one of the plastic laundry bags awaiting collection in the end utility room.

She sped down the corridor into Utility, her eye going at once to the area where the laundry bags were stacked. They weren't there, there was nothing there. With a sickening lurch of foreboding she remembered seeing the bags being removed by one of the porters at one o'clock, just after she got back from lunch. Panic gripped her. One o'clock . . . why, that was three hours ago! By now all Athelstone Ward's linen would be in one of the washers, in one of the huge washing machines that roared and pulsed and juddered in the laundry buildings just across the yard. She picked up the phone and dialled its number, and the manager answered her. 'Mr Cowes, can you tell me if Athelstone's laundry has gone into the washers yet?' She explained why she was asking. It had to be all right . . . it had to be! The charm had got to be found.

'I'll make enquiries. Hold on,' Arthur Cowes replied. Charis waited there, holding the phone, listening to the throb of the machines in the background, the sound of women's voices raised high above the din, the clashing sound of metal; until at last, at long last, after what was only minutes but seemed like hours, Arthur Cowes came back. 'You're in luck, it hadn't even been sorted, and I've got your little trinket, right here in the palm of my hand. I'll bring it up to you.'

Charis went to meet him—she couldn't wait, and in less than fifteen minutes the little St Christopher, washed and burnished, was back round Bernard Maxwell's neck. She told him it was there, so did his wife, but they couldn't be sure that he heard. The other nurses were told what had happened, and so was the SNO and the whole ward heaved a sigh of relief.

Charis stayed on duty. There was still much anxiety about Bernard Maxwell's condition; there was no sudden improvement once the charm was about his neck. Guy came up to the ward at six-thirty, when suppers were being served. He was still there at seven o'clock, but shortly after that Bernard Maxwell's temperature was well down, only one degree above normal; his b.p. was within reasonable limits, he was lucid and thirsty. He spoke to his wife, and he held the St Christopher between his thumb and forefinger. Not long after he was in a natural sleep.

'Do you think the charm made any difference?' Charis asked Guy in the office.

He shrugged and smiled. 'Who can possibly tell? I prefer to think it was us—your and my skills that caused him to rally again. On the other hand, the St Christopher plainly gives him peace of mind. He thinks it protects him, and who are we to scoff at his beliefs? Life is full of mysteries, Charis. I don't want them all unfolded. I like to feel there are sources of strength from which we can all draw in times of need . . . sources that never fail.'

'I know what you mean. I feel like that too.' She took off her cap, jerking at the grips, smoothing the wings of her hair.

'As I've said before, we think alike on many important issues.' There was something in his voice, in his seeking grey eyes, that made her catch her breath. The colour flowed in and out of her cheeks; she swallowed and reached for her cape. 'You're off home, are you?' He had opened the door and was standing half outside.

'Yes, I am. I'm very late, Helen will be worried.' She joined him in the corridor, and they travelled down in the lift, crossed the entrance hall together, emerged into the yard. Guy walked across to the cycle sheds with her.

'Is this your weekend off?' he asked.

She told him it was, 'And tomorrow Helen and I will be playing tourists. She never tires of the Cloisters Museum. I expect we'll end up there. She likes the section that has those casts of Greek and Roman sculpture. I do too, it reminds me of school. We used to be taken there to make sketches. It seems a long time ago.'

'Aeons of years, I've no doubt!' His expression was droll. She didn't know how to take him when he looked like that. He was a puzzling man, an enigma, like one of those mysteries he had talked about earlier; he was also a source of strength. She knew that instinctively, and as she smiled shyly up at him, he put an arm about her shoulder, turned her into him, and kissed her softly and warmly on the mouth.

'Charis, meaning grace,' he murmured, tracing the line of her brow. She stood there enchanted, entranced by his touch, then pulled away with a jerk as a group of students came chasing across the yard. 'Have a good weekend,' he said, turning away to the car park. Charis dragged her bicycle from the stand.

I could fall in love with him easily . . . easily, she thought. She cycled home like the wind, thrusting at the pedals, winging home on whirring, singing wheels. The evening sun lit a glow on her face to vie with the stars in her eyes. I could fall in love with him easily . . . easily. Perhaps I love him now. But

perhaps it's the spring, or a kind of fever, or a kind
of special madness that comes of kissing . . .

For Guy belonged to Joanne.

CHAPTER ELEVEN

THE rooms at the Cloisters Museum were relatively small. They were arranged with the individual taste one might expect from a private owner, rather than from a curator, who plainly took pride in his work. Persian and Turkish carpets enriched the polished floors, vases of flowers enhanced the beauty of rare chests and tables. The flowers on that May afternoon when Charis and Helen Keldos walked up the shallow stairs to view the first of the paintings were mauve and white stocks, Madonna lilies, spiked arrangements of broom; outside one of the high arched windows was an avenue of cherry trees in full bloom, pointing the way to the park.

'I meant to tell you,' said Helen, as they entered the first room, 'that I met Mr Morland this morning, buying a toothbrush in Boots. I told him we were coming here, and he seemed most interested. It would never surprise me if he turned up here, he was all on his own this morning. I may be wrong, but it struck me that he might be at a loose end.'

'His girl-friend's in London, that's why,' Charis told her, 'and he knew we were coming here, Helen. I told him so yesterday. I hope you didn't coerce him, press him to join us, or anything like that.'

'I like him.' Helen paused in front of a group of Florentine paintings. 'He's a kind man, dependable, the type to take care of a woman. What's his girl-friend like?'

'Dark and glamorous. She's also our Theatre Sister.'

'Eminently suitable, in other words. Let's hope she

makes him happy.' Helen's eyes slid from a painting
of Hector and Achilles to her granddaughter's face,
which was set in rigid lines.

They had been in the building nearly an hour when
Guy Morland arrived. By then they were on the
ground floor looking at pottery. Charis saw him first,
wending his way between the cabinets, his cream
sweater and fawn jeans a foil for his lean, dark looks.
Even in this, the rarefied atmosphere of the Cloisters
Museum, several heads were turning to look at him.

'I thought I'd take your advice and spend a couple
of hours in here,' he said, looking straight at Helen
Keldos, then more obliquely at Charis. 'I thought I
might persuade you to show me those Greek and
Roman casts.'

'You couldn't have anyone better than Charis, she's
sketched almost every one,' Helen said before Charis
could speak. 'You two go along. I'm going to find the
restaurant and sit down for a while.

'I'll come with you,' said Charis quickly, then felt
Guy's hand on her arm.

'I really would appreciate being taken to see those
casts.'

'They're across the garden in a separate building.'

'I think I can walk that far,' he said, half laughing,
and pretending to hobble along.

What could she do but laugh and give in, not so
much to his request as to her own wish to be with
him and stay at his side.

They saw Helen to the restaurant, then, leaving her
there, supplied with tea and toast, they crossed the
garden and made their way to the low stone building,
described in the Cloisters brochure as the Cave. 'I'm
sorry Helen let you in for this,' Charis said awkwardly.
'Much though I love her, there are times when . . . '

'Don't give it another thought. I'm never let in for
anything that I don't want to do myself—well, not
very often,' he qualified, and looking sharply at him,

she surprised a look of anxiety on his face. 'Come and show me your favourite pieces.' He opened the Cave door—a heavy door that clanged as they closed it to.

The gods stood all about them, ghostly white in the dimness—Hermes with the infant Dionysus, the Apollo Belvedere, the Venus de Milo, Hebe binding up her sandal, Artemis and Niobe, and many, many more. Charis, as she wandered amongst them with Guy at her side, felt as stirred as she had in her schooldays when, in her imaginings, she had released the gods from their wretched exile and made them free to wander wherever they pleased, forgetting their banishment.

It was something of a shock to re-emerge into the real world—into the blaze of the walled garden. They sat down on one of the seats . . . 'To get our breath back, to recover,' Guy said. Charis knew what he meant. And presently, as they sat there, feeling the sun's power, hearing the traffic sounds in the street, watching a feral cat sharpening its claws on the bark of a tree, they began to feel normal again—so normal that all Charis's awareness of the man sitting beside her returned full flood; she began to talk about work.

'Have you been to the Hospital this morning?' she asked. 'I was wondering about Mr Maxwell.'

'I have, and he's progressing satisfactorily, temp and pulse okay, there's very little swelling, no sign of infection, and his drain has been taken out. He's reasonably comfortable, cheerful as Larry, wanted to know where you were. Oh yes, and incidentally, that night nurse who scuttled his charm came up to find you this morning to say how sorry she was. She saw Peggy Barford, and I overheard part of their conversation.'

'It was good of her to come. It could have been my fault—that she rolled it up in his gown. I might not have fastened the chain properly . . . one thinks of all these things afterwards, and feels terrible.' Charis

fumbled in her bag, got out her dark glasses, and
thrust them on her nose.

'Any fault on your part was wiped out by your
brilliant detective work,' he said with a grin, hoping
to see her smile. But she didn't respond, and her face,
half hidden and dwarfed by the glasses, remained
remote and far away. He tried another tack. 'Tell me
about your grandmother's clinic.' He looked away
from her face to the yellow silken skirt of her dress,
fluttering softly sideways, filling the space between
them on the seat.

'It's a private orthopaedic clinic with three hundred
beds,' she explained. 'It was owned by my grandfather
and Helen jointly at first. When Grandfather died he
left Helen his share, so it's all hers now. Helen hopes,
very soon, to add a new wing and recruit more staff.
She acts as manager only now, doesn't nurse herself.
She's sixty-six, but I don't think she looks nearly that,
do you?'

'More like forty-five,' said Guy. 'You could pass
for mother and daughter. My parents are that age
exactly, my father's a GP in Wiltshire. My mother,
who abounds with energy, helps out on my brother's
farm. The farm practically adjoins the surgery, and
she divides her time between each. David declares he
could never cope with the paperwork without her.'

'Is David the brother who has the twin daughters?'

'That's right, yes . . . Lesley and Sue. It was
because of Sue, the precocious one, that you took me
for a thief, that day in Carter's store, remember?'

As if I could ever forget, thought Charis, going
peony-pink. He had all her attention now, he noticed.
She had snatched off her glasses and was staring
straight at him, willing him to explain.

'It all started,' he went on, 'when my mother, who's
Lesley's godmother, wanted to give her a special
necklace that had been in our family for years. It was
the twins' birthday on Christmas Eve, and she wanted

the necklace to be Lesley's present, she was very
determined on that. Then apparently Father, a peace-
loving man, pointed out to her that all hell would be
let loose if Sue didn't have one too. She's very spoiled,
I have to admit, she's pandered to far too much.
Nevertheless, Christmas being the season of goodwill,
my mother tried to ensure that peace would reign in
the Morland household by doing her best to buy
another blue necklace to match. She tried, but didn't
have any luck, so when I came here for my interview,
I volunteered to aid the search, to try the main shops
in Seftonbridge. Carter & Mayhews's was my first
port of call on that cold, bleak day, when a certain
young woman apprehended me!'

'What a fool I was!' sighed Cheris.

'Brave, I thought.'

'You didn't . . . not at the time!'

'Well, maybe not at the time,' he said, and she could
hear the smile in his voice. Turning her head, she
found him so close she could see herself reflected in
his long grey eyes that were shading to black. Then
his face blurred as he shifted to hold her, slewing
sideways on the seat. She felt the fan of his breath on
her cheek, saw the darkness of his head blot out the
sky before their lips met in a kiss of such intensity
that she seemed to melt and merge with him, become
the same person, fly with him to Olympus and
farther . . . fly with him to some planet where
nothing existed except emotion, where thinking had
no place. Even knowing that she loved him wasn't a
thought, it was part of the swirl of feeling that gave
her wings, that made her part of him. She came back
to earth when she heard his voice, when he moved
away from her, slowly away, sliding his hands down
the softness of her arms. 'Your grandmother is
descending upon us.' And she was. Charis turned and
saw her—pretty, sprightly Helen Keldos, looking about
forty, picking her way over the tussocky grass.

'If we're going to Nan's to supper, we ought to be making tracks,' she called when within a few feet of them; by then they were standing up. Guy was shading the sun from his eyes. Charis had found her dark glasses down in the grass and she put them back on her nose. Guy began to talk to Helen about the casts they had seen. His expression was guarded and he seemed determined to avoid looking at Charis. As they walked through the gates and stepped out into Princes Parade, she said, more in an attempt to gain his attention than anything else:

'You've still not told me if you managed to match that blue necklace.'

Helen was walking between them. He looked over her head as he said: 'No, *I* didn't, but Joanne did, two days before Christmas Eve. She found what was practically its twin in the Lanes at Brighton—her people live there. So all was well in the end.'

'Oh, good, I'm glad.' Charis managed to smile, while her heart plummeted. His mention of Joanne, coming then, was a jolting reminder that she existed, was the woman in his life. In all probability this afternoon had been nothing more than an interlude—a passing away of time till Joanne Tolbie arrived back from London. Perhaps he had just been feeling lonely . . . she choked on the coarser word, randy. As for her, she had shown her hand, he *must* know how she felt about him . . . and that terrible thought made her toes curl in her shoes. It was at that precise moment, as she lagged slightly behind, that she saw Neil in Hansons' forecourt, getting into his car. It was Saturday afternoon, but it was also the time of year when house properties were up for sale, and when would-be buyers abounded. At those times Neil worked all hours; he had been doing so today. He was off home now, but he spotted Charis, and her grandmother, and Guy Morland, on the other side of the railings, walking by. He recognised Helen, he had met her before on two of her visits to England. He left his car and ran out to meet her; they shook hands and exchanged a few words. Guy walked slowly on past Mathieson & Pratts, and looked in the window of an art gallery a few yards further on. Eventually Helen joined him, leaving Charis talking to Neil, or he to her.

'I was going to ring you,' he said. 'I've got two complimentary tickets for the Chopin recital next week. I thought we might go together, have supper first, perhaps. That is if you feel you'd like to come.'

'Which night is it?' she asked. He felt she was playing for time . . . time in which to couch an excuse for turning his invitation down. His eyes left hers and took in, a little way ahead, Mrs Keldos in her cotton print dress, beside her the lean-hipped figure of Guy Morland walking next to the kerb. The traffic was light this afternoon, most of the jams and pile-ups were in the main shopping centre. Princes Parade was quiet. Why was Morland with Charis and her grandmother? Had they met by chance? Surely Charis wasn't dating *him*. He dismissed the idea at once. They had probably met in the town somewhere. Yes, that was what it must be.

'The tickets are for Tuesday,' he told her. She was standing facing him, but looking at the pavement, tracing the dust with her shoe. Over her shoulder he could see a red bus trundling steadily nearer. A motorcyclist was trying to pass, he did so easily—a black leather Hell's Angel figure astride his heap of metal, snarling and zooming, swooping across the path of the laggard bus. He was showing off . . . showing his skills . . . showing off and losing control . . . losing control and flaring towards them, trying to straighten and failing . . . trying in vain, and mounting the pavement, rushing, rushing towards them . . . rushing at them, straight at them . . . *straight at them!* 'Charis!' Neil's shout was a scream, it tore from his throat at the same second that he grabbed her and threw her sideways . . . then the bike hit him; he felt himself flung in the air.

Charis, lying half stunned by the railings, couldn't move at first. She couldn't move, but she saw Neil lying on the ground. Farther along she saw the rider struggling to sit up, saw someone switch off and right his machine, saw the red side of the bus. Then Guy was in front of her, lifting her up, Helen just behind him. 'I'm all right, I'm all right!' She flung them off and pushed through to Neil. He was conscious, she saw his eyes, but he was breathing in catchy gasps. His face was grey, his legs drawn up, he was lying on his side. She saw Guy feel for his pulse, heard him shout to the crowd to stand back. Someone rang for an ambulance, and it came at once, swinging out of the Hospital gates less than a hundred yards up the road; it came silently towards them. Within ten minutes Neil and Tom Mayes, the terrified motorcyclist, were being wheeled into the Accident Bay.

Dr Pierce, the Casualty Officer, wasn't long examining Neil. He came out to Charis who was sitting in the waiting area with Helen and Guy. 'I'm as sure as I can be that his spleen's ruptured. I'm sending him straight up to Theatre. There's no time to lose, he's bleeding internally, they'll do all the prepping up there. He's been crossmatched and I've got him on a Dextran infusion. The rest, I'm afraid, is . . . not up to me.' He shook his head and frowned.

'May I see him, go up with him?' Charis lurched to her feet.

'Better not, my dear . . . better wait, I think. He's having breathing troubles. The best thing you can do is go home, and get some rest yourself.'

'Who's operating?' Guy cut in.

'Allan Bardwell, and who better? By a stroke of luck he was in the building, he's up in Theatres now.'

Charis heard Guy reply, heard him say something

about, 'fine surgeon' and 'couldn't have better' . . .
and 'didn't lose any time', but she was looking away
to the right-hand corridor, where a blanketed stretcher
trolley was being wheeled at speed towards the lifts.
A nurse was running alongside, holding a infusion
bottle; there was another nurse on the other side,
looking down at the patient. All Charis could see of
the patient was the top of his yellow fair head as it
lay on the pillow—Neil's head, Neil's hair; he had
probably saved her life. Was he going to lose his own?
'Oh, please let him be all right!' She didn't know she
had spoken aloud, till Helen and Guy, alarmed at her
pallor, pressed her down into a chair. But when Helen
suggested that they went home and telephoned in,
later on, she refused at once. 'No, Helen, I couldn't
possibly. I can't leave the building, there are things to
do, like ringing Neil's parents. They ought to know,
they'll want to come, and I must be here when they
do.'

With half her mind and attention she saw Guy and
Helen conferring. Then she felt Guy's hand on her
arm. 'I'll stay here with you,' he said. 'I'll just see Mrs
Keldos out, then we'll wait here together.'

She nodded, unable to speak, but she knew she
wanted him there. She had the feeling that with Guy
at her side the strength that his presence gave her
would somehow, in some way, convey itself to Neil,
struggling to survive up on the Theatre floor.

While Guy escorted Helen Keldos across the yard
to the gates, Charis was brought face to face with
Tom Mayes, the motorbike rider. His only injury,
apart from grazes and superficial bruising, was a
broken collarbone, which had been pulled into place
by a figure-of-eight bandage. As this would need to
be adjusted over the next few days, he was being
admitted into Athelstone Ward. Dr Pierce had told
him who Charis was and he came to speak to her.

'I'm sorry,' was all he said. He too was suffering from shock.

'I don't suppose you did it on purpose,' Charis said steadily. Guy and Helen, who had seen the accident quite plainly from where they stood, had said it looked as though Tom Mayes had been larking about and lost control of that dreadful bike, the roar of which Charis could still hear now. She didn't want to talk to the boy, and was glad when a young nurse arrived to take him up to the Ortho floor.

When she telephoned Neil's parents they said they would come at once. They got to the Hospital just before ten, by which time Neil was out of the theatre and in the recovery room. Allan Bardwell came down to see them. 'I've removed his spleen,' he said. 'Surgically he's fine, but I'm afraid he's suffering from severe haemorrhagic shock. We're countering this by continuous transfusion, which means that we have to watch, very carefully, the pressure on his heart.'

'Will he live?' Edgar Chambers asked bluntly. He was thickset and blond, like Neil.

'Unless complications set in, yes, I'm sure he will. Constitutionally he's strong, but severe shock is tricky, and your son lost a lot of blood. If you would like to stay the night in the hospital, we can fix you up with a room. You've probably travelled some distance.' His pale blue gaze took in Charis and Guy, as he spoke.

'We've come from Norwich.' Mrs Chambers' face, always dark and peaky, and a little swarthy, took on a haunted look. 'I think we ought to stay,' she said, and her husband agreed with her. Embracing Charis and telling her to go home and get some rest, they went to the lifts with Sister Casualty, who took them to the wing on the second floor reserved for overnight guests.

'Come on now, I'm taking you home, and no arguments,' said Guy, removing from Charis's lap a tray of coffee and sandwiches, which she'd scarcely touched. The food and drink sickened her.

'Yes—all right, yes, I'll come. Now that Neil's parents are here, I don't feel I'm leaving him to fight it out on his own.' She shuddered as she rose to her feet, and he made her wear his sweater, easing it over her ruffled head, pushing her arms in the sleeves and rolling the cuffs up over her wrists. 'So I'm wearing the Emperor's new clothes again, am I?' The sweater was warm from his body, it warmed hers, as she sank down into it.

'You're under Emperor's orders too!' He picked up her shoulder bag, took her arm and marched her to the doors.

In his car outside, in the comfortable seat, belted tightly in, lassitude claimed her, swamped her in waves; it was difficult to talk. Her lids felt weighted, so did her limbs; the street lamps and traffic headlights appeared at chinks, annoying glints, when all she craved was darkness, and the chance to sleep, the car's purr lulled her, she couldn't keep awake. 'I'm sorry—I just—I couldn't help it,' she muttered, as her head dropped forward, and the jerk woke her up, and she saw Guy looking at her.

'You're home, little one, you can sleep all you like, once I get you inside.'

But now she was wide awake and her mind was crowding with thoughts of Neil. 'Guy, before we go in, what do you really think about Neil? He'll get well, he'll make it, won't he?' The seat belt flew back from her hand. 'Mr Bardwell said he was strong constitutionally, so that's bound to be in his favour. If he dies, I don't know what I'll do. It was me he . . . me he saved. If he'd thought of himself when he saw that motorbike charging towards us, he'd have been all right. *I* would have been where *he* is now, tied up to drips, fighting for my life.'

'He won't die.' Guy's hand gripped hers, then as quickly relinquished it.

'I shall go in tomorrow, first thing, and see for myself how he is,' Charis went on.

'You think a lot of him, don't you?'

She turned and saw his face—near, but not close, the difference was subtle, but she felt it, even then. The magnetism that had drawn them together that afternoon on the seat wasn't working now, wasn't there now; too much had happened since. 'Yes, I think a lot of him, I've known him for a long time,' she said shakily, as he helped her out of the car.

Helen had the front door open and behind her in the hall Charis could see Nan and Harold. Nan came out and dragged her inside. 'We decided to reverse the supper arrangement and come here to you, when we heard what had happened. Oh, you poor love, it must have been terrible!'

Helen asked Guy in, but he shook his head. 'I'd better get home,' he said. 'Charis needs to rest, needs her family around her.'

'Well, she's certainly got that,' said Helen, jerking her head back towards Nan, who was bundling Charis up the stairs to bed. 'Thank you for looking after her,' she added more equably, standing at the door until he had driven away.

CHAPTER TWELVE

WHEN Neil started talking about compensation Charis knew he was getting better. The relief was enormous, for the past three days had been crucial and anxious ones. Because of extensive bruising to his chest he had found breathing difficult. On the Sunday after surgery his left lung had collapsed. He had been very ill and the Chambers had stayed on, living with Charis and Helen at Cranleigh. But now, apart from troublesome hiccups, not uncommon with diaphragm bruising, Neil was doing well and talking money; his parents had gone back home. 'I shall make a claim, I'd be a fool not to,' he whispered to Charis, when during her lunch break on the Thursday after the accident, she went along to Edgbaston Ward to take him some magazines.

'You can think about that when you're stronger, Neil.' He still looked pallid and ill. His hair had darkened, his cheeks had hollowed, and she fancied there were wrinkles about his eyes that hadn't been there before.

'I could have a word with Peter Trueman, he's still in your ward, isn't he?'

'He is, but he won't be walking around for another two weeks,' she said, 'and he certainly won't be coming down here, nor will you be making trips up. Wait until you're discharged, Neil, you can do all your business then.'

'Mayes' insurance company will cough up,' Neil said wearily. Talking tired him more than he realised. Maybe Charis was right. He wasn't strong enough,

not yet, but once he was out of here . . . He sighed,
but not too deeply; movement made his stitches drag.
Whoever would have thought that this would happen
to him of all people? It didn't occur to him—why
should it?—that for the first time in his life he had
acted on impulse, without thinking, and come out the
worse for it.

Back on Athelstone Ward Charis was just in time
to see Tom Mayes, who was going home with his
father, his shoulders still tightly braced. 'Another
fortnight should see you right, Tom, but keep those
bandages tight,' she cautioned his father, smiling at
them both. 'This type of fracture is always a nuisance,
the bandages cause chafing, due to their rigidity,
however well they're applied.'

'It'll teach him to be more careful, Nurse,' Mr
Mayes said sourly. This wasn't the first time Tom had
come to grief on his motorbike. 'It seems to me the
young never learn,' he added even more aggrievedly.

'Sorry' and 'Thanks' were Tom's jerked-out words,
as his father led him away.

'He doesn't get much sympathy from Dad, does
he?' Guy Morland stared after them. He had come to
the ward to do a short round before his outpatients'
clinic. 'You were very forbearing, very good with him;
it couldn't have been that easy.'

'It's called being detached,' smiled Charis. 'I had to
forget what he did. And Neil is noticeably better
today, I've just been down to see him. Margaret
Brodie will be going in later on, and I know Nan and
Helen will. Now that he can see people, he'll soon
pick up.'

'I'm sure he will. I saw him myself, for a few
minutes,' said Guy. 'He's talking of having work sent
in, which is usually a good sign. And talking of work,
let's do some, shall we?' He swept into the office, and
she followed him, feeling a shade rebuffed. He was
probably, she thought, sick to death of Neil and the

accident. He had done his part, he had sympathised, reassured and supported her. Now he wanted to get on with his work, and who could blame him for that? The breeze from the open window fluttered some papers off the desk. She bent to retrieve them, and as she straightened she saw him by the filing cabinets, leaning over one of the pulled-out drawers. 'If you're ready,' he said, 'can you find me some notes? I want to see Maxwell and Trueman, and Giles Barry, and then I'll have to be off.' He didn't sound exactly impatient, and his tone was pleasant enough, but he didn't turn and meet her eye, he seemed to be gazing unseeingly at the rows of folders, and pushing them back and forth.

'The notes are at the ward desk.' She ought to say 'Mr Morland', but she couldn't, the title stuck in her throat.

'Oh, of course they are.' He shut the drawer. 'I must be losing my grip.' Even then he studiously avoided looking in her direction. He made for the door and held it open, then smiled effusively at Peggy Barford, who was passing with some sheets.

They followed Peggy into the ward. She and Nurse Varden were going to make up Dick Rosen's vacant bed. Dick had been discharged and a patient for arthroplasty would be coming in tomorrow at ten o'clock.

Giles Barry's restricting hip spica had been removed that morning and for the first time in five weeks he was able to sit up in bed. 'Tomorrow I'll have that pin out,' Guy told him, inspecting it. 'You'll have an injection, a local anaesthetic, so you won't feel anything. After that, in gradual stages, we'll get you mobile again.'

'So the worst is over, is it?' Mr Barry's paper-thin face creased into a smile of relief,

'The hard work is yet to come. The rest is largely up to you and the physiotherapy team.' After exam-

ining the state of his skin, and asking a question or
two, Guy left the bedside. 'I'll remove that pin
tomorrow afternoon. I'm in theatre all morning,' he
told Charis, as he scribbled in the notes.

Peter Trueman enquired how Neil was. 'Getting on
well now, thanks,' Charis answered briefly, conscious
of Guy standing by to examine Peter's arm. He too
had had his plaster taken off that morning. He
complained of a feeling of weakness in the arm.

'I feel afraid to use it,' he confessed.

'Don't be,' Guy assured him. 'X-Ray have confirmed
a good union of both forearm bones. They were stable
fractures, there was no displacement, which makes
things easier. You should be able to manipulate a
walking frame all right.'

'It'll be my leg I'll be wary of then,' said Peter,
looking glum. Now that at long last he was ready to
walk, he found himself dreading it. I feel just like a
ship about to be launched, he thought, as he reached
for his comb and tidied himself ready for Claire, who
was coming at visiting time. She would set him to
rights, she always did, she jollied him along. What he
would do without her he couldn't think.

Bernard Maxwell, the amputee patient, was going
through the stage of feeling that he still had his right
'bad' leg. 'I find myself looking down the bed and
expecting to see it,' he said. 'When I wake in the
night, I'm certain it's there. You warned me of this, I
know. Phantom leg's the right term for it, and it's
downright uncanny. I never thought the feeling would
be so strong.'

'I'm sorry, but there's nothing we can do about it,'
Guy told him quietly. 'It might go on for weeks, even
months, and even then it won't go at once, not *all* at
once, you'll 'lose' the leg in parts. With a mid-thigh
amputation like yours, you'll feel that your knee has
gone first, then your shin, then your foot and toes.'

He examined the stump. 'How are you getting on with your exercises?'

'I do them, or try to . . . bit of an effort.'

'You'll feel better once your stitches are out. We'll probably decide to remove them over two consecutive days, starting next Thursday, perhaps.' Guy watched Charis replace the cradle and arrange the bedclothes on top.

'I can hardly wait,' Bernard Maxwell said, managing to smile. All in all, things weren't too bad. At least he was out of pain. To be free of pain from that no-good leg was a bonus in itself. He would soon get used to a false one; other people did. It was never too late to learn a new trick, and I've always been one for a challenge, he told himself, settling down for a nap.

'His foot needs attention,' said Guy, when they got back into the office.

'If you mean that his nails want trimming, I know,' Charis answered quickly. 'I've been two nurses short for the last three days, but I've asked the chiropodist to attend to him. He'll come after visiting.'

'I wasn't finding fault, just pointing out a fact.' He went to the window and closed it against a sudden shower that blew in, spotting the sill. 'The ward has been very well run in Sister Holt's absence. You've been, and are being, very efficient. When one has private worries, it makes the job that much more difficult.'

'It helped, being extra busy,' she said, pleased enough with the praise, but it wasn't what she wanted from him; she *knew* she had run the ward well; other people had told her that, including the SNO What she wanted was for him to unbend, just for a minute or two, drop his cool professionalism, look at her with liking, at the very least, and say something personal. She was hoping, and looking, and watching for crumbs, and she ought to have more pride, and more sense too. She felt cold and miserable. 'All the same, I'll be glad to see Sister Holt back on Saturday,' she said as he signed the prescriptions on the desk.

'I'm going on leave myself tomorrow night, just for one week . . . to my parents in Wiltshire.' He pushed the prescriptions towards her.

'That's very sudden,' Charis blurted out, before she could stop herself.

'I had to fit it in with my theatre list, which is short next week.' He was clipping his Biro back on his pocket, making movements to leave.

'You'll be glad of a rest,' she remarked.

'Of a change, at least. I'll be here tomorrow to see the new man Patrick Royle, before I set off. His notes should be coming up from Records later this afternoon. And now I must go, or I'll have them queueing up for me downstairs. What it is to be sought after!' And yes, he smiled at her then, over his shoulder en route for the corridor.

Charis moved to the window and stood looking out, her feeling of loneliness intensified by the wet and blustery grey scene below. The way Guy had been, his arms length treatment, was partly, she knew, because they were both on duty, but equally she was sure he had been deliberately showing her that enough was enough; he didn't want to get involved any more than he was. Sister Tolbie was back. Charis and Helen had seen her yesterday. She had been in Guy's car, coming down from the station, as they had halted at the lights. It had been impossible not to notice their absorption with one another. Helen had agreed that Joanne was lovely, 'But looks aren't everything,' she said with a sharp glance at her granddaughter.

Next day, Friday, Guy was operating up until one-thirty. When he made his way to Athelstone Ward in the late afternoon, Charis was with the SNO, who wanted to talk to her about the re-opening of two of the side wards, which had recently been re-plumbed. Peggy Barford dealt with Guy, who left for Warminster a good half an hour before Charis got back to the ward.

'It's all right, Peggy, I didn't need to see him,' she said as she drank the tea that Jane Adams had brought in for her; it went down her throat in gulps. She spent the next hour before off-duty time making out requisitions for the side ward equipment Miss Jay had spoken about.

On the day before Guy was due back from Wiltshire, Peter Trueman was discharged. Claire Spalding came to fetch him, looking just as belligerent as she had on the very first day she had come to the ward and tipped Melissa Ivyson off her chair. Charis wheeled Peter out to the lifts, Rob carried his walking frame, while Claire Spalding brought up the rear, wearing baggy cotton trousers and a clinging vest with rows of golden chains.

'You're invited to the wedding in four weeks' time,' Peter said at the lifts. 'Yes, I do mean both of you, and bring Neil too, of course, that is if he's well enough.'

'He's going home today,' said Charis as the lift settled itself to a floating halt and Peter, still issuing invitations, was wheeled inside by a frowning, black-browed Claire. The lift went down, and Rob turned to Charis.

'You can never tell,' he said, 'what it is that brings two people—male and female—together. That girl's not even attractive!'

'She is to him,' Charis laughed.

'You coming to lunch?' Rob asked her, nodding towards the stairs.

'I'm having it with Neil in Edgbaston Ward, out on the colonnade—special permission from Sister Miller; Neil wangled it,' she told him. 'His parents are coming at two o'clock and taking him back to Norwich for three weeks, till he gets really fit again.'

'Sounds the best thing. See you later, then.' Rob

took the stairs at a run. Charis walked down to the
first-floor surgical wards. She found Neil dressed and
out on the long glassed-in balcony, referred to by the
staff as 'the colonnade'. A small folding table had
been opened up and set in front of him; he was reading
the menu sheet as Charis approached.

'It's tongue and salad, and honeycomb pudding,
whatever that is,' he said. 'They're bringing it out here
to us.'

'Oh, I'll fetch it. The trolleys have just been wheeled
into the ward. I can't let the nurses wait on me, Neil,
I'd feel absolutely awful.' She went into the ward and
came out with two loaded trays. 'There you are,
cutlery as well!' She arranged the food on the table.

'You're a far nicer person than me, I'd have sat
here and let them bring it,' said Neil, accepting a
paper napkin and spreading it out on his knees.

'You're entitled to be waited on, you're the patient.'

'Not for much longer, though. I know I've got to
go home,' he said. 'I could hardly go back to my digs,
but I would rather have stopped in Seftonbridge, all
my contacts are here.'

Charis felt a prick of compunction, not very far
short of guilt. Nan had wanted her to have Neil at
Cranleigh, to let him convalesce there. 'Darling, after
what he did for you, after all he's been through, I
can't help feeling you ought to have him, it's the very
least you can do. Helen's a nurse, and so are you, it'd
be the perfect set-up.' Nan had been hopeful that this
would bring Neil and Charis together again. But
Charis, not daring to look at Helen, had very quickly
said that Neil's parents wanted him at home.

'I can't possibly interfere with that,' she had told
her sister seriously. 'If we were still engaged it might
be different, but we're not, which makes it tricky. I
shall never forget what he did, Nan, never, but to
have him here wouldn't be fair.' She looked to Helen
for backing, but her grandmother didn't give it, at

least not in words, but Charis was sure she understood how she felt, and respected her feelings, and agreed with her as well. And quite apart from anything else, Helen was on holiday. It was hardly fair to lumber her with a semi-invalid. Nan had looked cross; she was always twitchy when Helen came to England. Why she should be Charis couldn't for the life of her imagine. She supposed it was one of those inexplicable clashes of personality which arose in most families from time to time.

'Three weeks will soon go, Neil,' she said encouragingly, glad to see him tackling his food, plainly enjoying his lunch.

'You're probably right, I dare say it will.' He seemed disinclined to talk. He was the kind of man who preferred to get the business of eating done first, and *then* talk; he disliked doing both at once.

From where they were sitting, near to the glassed-in side of the balcony, they could see the tide of traffic sweeping down Princes Parade. The green-domed roof of the Cloisters Museum was plainly visible. Charis looked at it and immediately thought of Guy. What was he doing right at this moment, and when would he be back? On Monday, she supposed; and then she thought of something that Dilys had said. Rumour had it, according to Dilys, that Morland and Tolbie had quarrelled. They had had a bust-up, which was why he'd got leave and departed at such short notice. It was also why, just for once in her life, the efficient Sister Tolbie was looking just a shade less pleased with herself.

After lunch and over the donkey brown liquid that the catering staff called coffee, Neil leaned over the rickety table and took Charis's hand in his. 'Can't you and I,' he said earnestly, 'begin all over again? I wanted to ask you weeks ago, that night we found the will, but I didn't like to, I felt it would look as though I was muscling in. Even now doesn't seem the right time, either, because you're bound to think I'm using the fact that I saved your life as a sort of bargaining point. I'm not, though.' He broke off; weakness was making him sweat. 'I love you, you see,' he added quickly, watching her face, which told him nothing, except that she was distressed. So was he, yet if she refused him, he would stand it, he supposed. He wasn't the sort to consider the world well lost for love. Even so, he had feelings.

Charis knew this and hated herself. 'Dear Neil, it wouldn't work out. It wasn't working before, not really, we both know it wasn't. Fondness and friendship isn't enough to base a marriage on.'

'It is for me.'

'But not for me . . . don't you see how different we are?'

'That's your final word?'

'It has to be.'

'Well, there's one thing that's certain,' he said, 'I shall never marry anyone else. In a way it's a relief to realise that, since I know which direction to take. Everything changed when your father died—his death was the turning point. We're all facing different ways now, whether we like it or not.'

An auxiliary nurse came out to collect their cups and fold up their table. She was followed by Sister, who told Neil that his parents had arrived. Charis went with Neil to meet them, then down to the waiting car. 'Good luck, and God bless,' she said as she kissed him and helped him into the back, watched by Mrs Chambers, who had never really thought that Charis would make the sort of wife she wanted for her son. He needed someone older, someone businesslike, someone less romantic who would help him get on, and further his career.

It was perfectly true what Neil had said, Charis thought, as they drove away. Since her father's death, so many things had changed.

Guy Morland arrived back earlier than expected. Charis saw his car on the parking space when she went off duty three hours later. She stopped still, staring at it, aware of her racing heart. There had been no sign of him in the building; perhaps he had merely called in on his way back from Wiltshire, before going home to his flat. There were several people crossing the yard, this being the time of day when the early shift nurses, like herself, were coming out in droves. Joanne Tolbie was one of them. She came running down the steps, still in her white uniform dress, her mass of curly hair imprisoned on top, skewered into a bun. At first Charis thought she was coming her way, towards the bicycle sheds, but no, she cut off diagonally in the direction of Guy's car. Charis watched her stop by it, unlock the door, swing it open wide. She was going to get inside and wait for him, she was going home with him. But Joanne wasn't getting into the car, she was leaning forward into it, picking something up from one of the seats. It looked like a sweater or cardigan, she was hanging it over her arm and re-locking the car, her dark head slightly bent. Then someone called to her, hailed her from a short distance off. Turning her eyes, Charis saw Leigh Stanton striding towards Joanne, and she heard what he said as plainly as though he shouted the words in her ear. 'Jo, hello! I've just seen Guy. I hear congrats are in order!'

'Yes, they are!' Joanne laughed, going forward to meet him. He shook her hand, then gave her a hug, and their words were lost to Charis, who stood there watching, as though she were glued to the ground. As Leigh Stanton moved off, Joanne looked up and saw her, waved, and began to walk in her direction. She looked jaunty and smiling and pleased. As she drew nearer Charis could see that the garment she carried was the cream sweater Guy had worn that afternoon at the Museum; it was the one he had wrapped her

in, made her put on, the night Neil had been so ill.
Facing Joanne at close range now, she found she was
stuck for words. Why had Leigh Stanton congratulated her? Was she marrying Guy? Had something
been decided, brought to a head, during his precipitate
absence? Had the row they were supposed to have
had cleared the air for good?

Joanne transferred the sweater from her arm to
about her shoulders. She tied the sleeves loosely, then
rubbed her face against the soft fine wool. The action
was deliberate and, to Charis, significant. Seeing it,
she felt knifed. It was true then, really true; their affair
had been serious, leading to marriage . . . *he was
going to marry her*.

'Aren't you going to take a leaf out of Leigh's
book?' Joanne was saying. 'Congratulations are the
order of the day, Guy's spreading the news right round
the block at this moment. It's no secret, you know.
You needn't be bashful!' She laughed, showing perfect
teeth. Charis stared at them, at the smiling mouth;
she couldn't see anything else.

'Congratulations, I wish you happiness.' She forced
out the stilted words.

'Thanks,' Joanne said carelessly. 'Being settled makes
such a difference.' And then she went off, swinging
her hips, holding the sweater in place, triumph in
every line of her lissom form.

'Tell me to mind my own business, if you like,'
Helen Keldos remarked after supper, 'but I can see
there's something wrong, Charis, and if you want to
talk, I'm ready to listen.' Helen was sewing, she was
making a pure silk shirt from a remnant she'd bought
at Carter & Mayhew's two days ago. With the soft
material loose in her fingers she looked at her granddaughter's face, noting her restless movements as she
sat stroking Homer's head. 'Is it Neil, my darling?'

'No, not Neil.'

'I think he wants you back.'

'He does, but I can't . . . he knows that. I've told him,' Charis answered in jerks. 'I'm in love with Guy Morland—I have been for ages. I think that's partly why I broke my engagement, although I didn't realise that at the time. I don't think . . . he was never . . . he didn't feel the same . . . Guy didn't, I mean. He's going to marry Joanne Tolbie, I've just seen her, and she told me so. She was so pleased . . . she was *gloating*, Helen! Oh, Helen, I can't bear it!' Sliding down on to the rug and burying her face in Homer's neck, she burst into tears, into harsh sobs, over which she had no control. So much had been pent up, dammed up, for so long—perhaps since her father died; she had been dry-eyed then, so perhaps she cried for all sorts of reasons, but every reason led back to Guy, and she knew she had loved him since the day she had drawn the sketch and seen his anger and his hurt, and had hated herself, and loved him . . . and kept on loving him. 'Bawling my head off isn't going to help,' she said, sitting up at last, blowing her nose with such vigour and noise that Homer beat a retreat. The most unlikely noises upset him, nose-blowing was one of them. Helen pressed a glass of brandy into her hand.

'I saw the attraction between the two of you that first day,' she said, 'on the day I came to England and he ran us home in his car. I'm surprised he's marrying the Tolbie girl, suitable though she may be. I thought . . . ' but at that point she stilled her tongue, deciding not to mention that she had seen Charis and the handsome Guy locked in each other's arms on the seat in the Cloisters garden, two weeks ago. Then when she had talked and walked with him along Princes Parade afterwards, she could have sworn that he had been huffed and worried when Charis stopped with Neil. Still, you could never tell with men, she might have misread the signs. Drat the man! Her heart ached for Charis, all her protective instincts started to

march forward, but she pushed every one of them
back. Charis was adult. Let Nan do the mothering, if
she liked. Not for the first time Helen had a nasty and
very shaming suspicion that she might be just a little
jealous of Nan.

'If things get too tough for you, there'll be a vacancy
at my clinic at the end of July. It's a Sister's post, and
yes, you could fill it, you're more than up to the job.
It's my own clinic, I appoint whom I please, so it
would save me advertising. It would also save me
getting someone whom I don't know and may not
like.'

Charis sipped her brandy, hating the smell, but
liking the spread of warmth that settled inside her and
steadied her; she felt she had passed through a storm.
'You're offering me a bolthole, Helen,' she sighed.

'What I'm offering you,' said Helen, 'is a worthwhile
job in a beautiful country with excellent pay and
conditions, and a warm climate—at least for most of
the year.'

'I love it here, I love Seftonbridge,' but even as she
spoke Charis thought of Guy and Joanne married, of
having to meet and see them as a married couple, see
Guy as a married man. 'To leave would be running
away,' she added.

'In a sense I suppose it would, but it wouldn't seem
like that to others. It would look entirely natural for
you to want to nurse in my clinic, in a country that's
partly your own. Greece and its beautiful islands are
part of your heritage, Charis.'

'I know.'

'So think about it, that's all I ask at this stage. And
whatever you decide, I'm on your side, that's what
grandmas are for!' Put like that it sounded so funny
that Charis had to laugh. Her emotions were close to
the surface this evening, laughter and tears ran hand-
in-hand, neither was very far off.

It was getting light before she finally got to sleep

that night. In less than an hour after that the milk-
man's float whined down the lane. It woke her up to
the realisation—all over again—that to put Guy out
of her thoughts and her life she would have to leave
Seftonbridge. But Greece—she didn't know. There
was Nan and Harold, she would hardly ever see them.
Perhaps she could get a post in London, or even in
Oxfordshire. This was her weekend off, so when she
was shopping later this morning she would get a copy
of the *Nursing Times* and see what was advertised.

In the end it was Helen who did the shopping, for
just after nine o'clock a removals van arrived to take
some items of furniture to Nan at the Nurseries.
Charis saw it come up the drive. 'It's to take the stuff
that belonged to Nan's mother,' she explained to
Helen. 'I shall have to see it out, I'm afraid. I'd
completely forgotten it.'

'You've had other things on your mind,' said Helen,
going to fetch her coat.

Greeting the men, restraining Homer, Charis tore
about the house putting stickers on the pieces of
furniture—most of them antique—that had belonged
to the first Mrs Littleton and had been at Cranleigh
House for most of the time that Nan had lived at
home. The men were the ponderous, slow-moving
kind; they were still at the house when Helen got
back, and because of the van taking up most of the
drive, Charis had no idea that Helen had returned in
Guy's car till she appeared in the front hall, climbing
over furniture, telling her that Guy was helping the
men load a sideboard into the van. 'But . . . Helen!'
was all she could say.

'And I've asked him in for coffee.'

'Oh, you haven't . . . you can't have!' Charis
stared at Helen aghast. Surely her grandmother knew
that she couldn't just sit down and be sociable . . .
entertain him! What on earth was she thinking about?

'And you're wrong about him,' Helen went on.

'You must have got things muddled. I congratulated
him on his engagement and he looked at me in
amazement. The Tolbie girl is *leaving*, not marrying
him, she's got another job—a Theatre Sister's job in
London; that's why she was cock-a-hoop. Charis, how
could you possibly have thought . . . ' She broke off
as Guy appeared, tall and lean in the doorway, wearing
one of his dark grey suits. Looking at him, Charis
had a sense of travelling back in time. He had looked
very much like this on the first day she had met
him . . . formally met him . . . when he came up
to the ward. But she was still trying to make sense of
what Helen had said—Sister Tolbie was leaving . . .
there was no engagement . . . so were they parting
for good? The thought of that turned her dizzy, while
normal conventional behaviour prompted her to ask
him about his holiday, and enquire about the weather
in the West Country, and ask how things were on the
farm.

Helen barked her shin on an oak settle. 'Oh, look,
you two,' she cried, 'why don't you go through into
the kitchen? I'll see the furniture out, and take Homer
with you, he's getting that crafty look in his eye which
means he's going to take a snap at the next leg he sees
feeling its way backwards down the stairs. I prefer not
to see it happen.' All but driving them into the kitchen,
she closed the door and left them on their own.

Charis looked at Guy. 'I'm sorry,' she said, 'Helen
is inclined to be bossy. It's the Matron in her coming
out. Sit down, I'll make the coffee.' Pulling out a chair
from the centre table, she made for the line of
cupboards on the opposite wall, and reached for the
coffee jar.

'I like your grandmother,' Guy said lightly, not
sitting down on the chair, but standing with his back
to the window, looking over at her. 'I have to admit
that she startled me, though, on our way back here,

by wishing me all the very best on my forthcoming marriage!'

'I'm sorry, that was my fault.' Charis spooned coffee grounds into the percolator basket with a none too steady hand. 'I thought you were getting married to Joanne, I'm afraid I made a mistake. I heard Dr Stanton congratulating her, and I jumped to the wrong conclusion. Your name was mentioned, and it all seemed to fit.' She decided not to tell him that Joanne had deliberately led her to make that particular jump. Yet why had she? What was the point? Because she must, reasoned Charis, have known that I'd find out the truth quite soon, so why go through all that charade? It could only be that she wanted to give me a hard time for a few hours, because she knows, or at any rate suspects how I feel about Guy. She was watching points, seeing how I'd react.

'She's got a Theatre Sister's post at the Walbrook,' said Guy, sitting down. 'We both worked there at one time, in our salad days, as you might say. She helped me pick up the pieces after I was jilted by a girl I very much wanted to marry. Joanne can be kind. She can also,' he added, 'be exceedingly spiteful, but we're none of us perfect, are we?'

'No, that's very true, we're not.' Charis joined him at the table.

'We lost touch after I moved to Warminster. I didn't know she'd come here, but when I applied for my post with Sir Rodney, she wrote to me, wishing me luck. I thought it was very nice of her, and I wasn't exactly displeased to know that *if* I got the job, there would be someone here I knew. I even began to wonder if we might end up married. I wanted a home, family life, all the things that marriage brings. But,' he moved his hands expressively, 'it didn't work out that way. On the work front . . . yes, marvellous. On a personal level, no. There was friendship, of course, but very little else. I was relieved when she told me she was applying for a senior post at the Walbrook, but when she came back after the interview, she was certain it had gone badly. For the first time ever I saw her really down. Still, she got it, landed the post, heard the good news by telephone yesterday afternoon, and I ran slap into all the excitement when I called in on my way back from holiday. Then I got caught up in a crisis in Casualty; it was midnight before I got home. Joanne, by the way, leaves at the end of June.'

The coffee percolator had been making its rhythmic lumping sound for some time—like a heart, Charis thought, like my own heart beating . . . bump-lump . . .   bump-lump . . .   bump-lump . . . bump-lump. She felt she would suffocate.

'I hear Neil has gone home, and that you turned down his *re*-offer of marriage.' Guy looked at her straightly, and she felt her colour rise.

'Helen has filled you in pretty well,' she observed, with an edge to her voice.

'Yes . . . well, I happen to know he was going to ask you again. He gave me to understand that, when I saw him in the ward. He said you'd only split up through a silly sort of tiff, that you were confused and very upset at the time your father died. I got the very firm impression that Neil was warning me off.'

'Oh, I don't think . . . ' Charis stared at him.

'I'm sure of it,' he snapped. 'And now I learn you're seriously thinking of going to work in Greece! Surely deciding not to marry Chambers doesn't warrant that, doesn't make such an abyss in your life that you have to emigrate!'

He was nervous, she realised . . . angry-nervous. He didn't want her to go. Looking back into his furious face, trying to see beyond it, she knew she had reached a time of total crisis in her life. 'Nothing has been decided,' she said firmly, 'but if I leave Sefton-bridge, it won't be because of Neil, *he* hasn't unsettled me. I'm fond of him in perhaps the same way that you are fond of Joanne, but he shouldn't have made the point that I was confused when Father died. I was confused at the time we got engaged, not when we split up.'

The coffee pot switched itself off, and she got up to fill the cups, but before she could do so Guy came up behind her and turned her round to face him. 'Charis, that afternoon . . . in the Museum garden . . . I wanted to tell you then what I felt, to tell you that I loved you.' His eyes were tender, anxious, searching, but he made no move to hold her, neither did she move closer to him, just listened to his words—'Yes, I wanted to tell you that afternoon how much you meant to me,' he smiled faintly, touching the side of her face. 'But your grandmother came on us over-suddenly, and the moment was lost. I was determined to retrieve it, though, by asking you out to supper—a candlelit supper, all the trimmings. I was busy planning it as we walked along Princes Parade, then we saw Neil in Hanson's yard. You stopped with him, I walked on with Helen, then that motorbike mounted the pavement. When I saw what nearly happened to you . . . saw what Chambers did, and what happened to him, I knew that whatever I felt and wanted to say was going to have to be put under wraps. I was almost an interloper, or I felt I was, during most of that time.'

'That's not true . . . I couldn't have got through it if you hadn't been with me, Guy!' Charis shivered and he caught her to him, laying her head on his chest, resting his cheek against her hair.

'During all that week, afterwards, I was sure I'd lost you to Neil. I felt that what I'd had for a time, or *thought* I'd had for a time, had slipped from my grasp, and wouldn't come back again.'

'But I've loved you for a long time.' She moved to look up at him. 'I think I started to love you that day

I drew the sketch; it came out so easily, as though you'd been in my head and my heart for ever.'

Guy groaned; she heard him. 'My dearest girl . . . my darling girl of grace!' He covered her face with little kisses, kisses that closed her eyes, drifted softly over her ears, smoothed the curve of her throat. 'I love you so much, you can't know how much, you mean the whole world to me.' His voice was thick and rough with emotion, his features blurred and close, his breath was warm—a caress in itself. 'Are you going to marry me?'

'Yes, Guy . . . oh, yes, of course!' Her arms went round his neck, then his mouth met hers . . . and both of them were lost.

The comments on their forthcoming marriage, set for the first of July, were numerous and various, and interesting to hear.

Helen was thrilled, but not surprised. 'I could see it coming,' she said. Privately she thought that with any luck, long before she was seventy, Guy and Charis might make it their business to make *her* a great-grandmother—something she could boast about for years.

Nan was astounded. 'You kept that dark!' she laughed, kissing Charis warmly. 'But, my darling, I couldn't be more pleased. Guy's a charming man.' Harold, all smiles, agreed with her; he had so much hoped that Charis wouldn't go back to Neil; he was too cautious by half. Charis was young and vibrant and tender, like some of his best plants. Guy Morland would take good care of her.

Dilys hugged her friend and said: 'Wow!' Rob Peele looked embarrassed. As for Joanne, she said very little when Guy was with Charis, but one day when she saw her alone, she made the pithy comment that living in the provinces wasn't for her.

As luck would have it, Charis saw Neil during the

third week in June, soon after he had got back from Norwich. He looked amazingly well. He had seen the engagement notice in the paper. 'I meant to write,' he told her, 'but then I thought I'd be bound to see you. I wish you happiness.' Then almost in the same breath he told her that his father had agreed to guarantee him a loan, enabling him to negotiate for the lease of the office premises in Kingsford. 'The ones Hansons pulled out of. I'm setting myself up in business, Charis, I'll be my own boss. I intend to call it Chambers & Co. I shan't have much staff at first, but Margaret is coming with me . . . coming *in* with me, I mean. She'll do all the secretarial work, manage things, you know. She's been very unhappy at Hansons since your father died.' He didn't mention that Margaret, too, had made him a sizeable loan. She had sold the painting of the horses. 'Mr Littleton would have approved, he had great faith in you, Neil, just as I have.' Neil was gratified. He had always felt that Margaret was on his side.

So Charis and Guy were married on a brilliant July day. Harold gave the bride away, while Guy's brother was best man, and his daughters, the twins, made a pair of pretty bridesmaids. They wore dresses of broderie anglaise, threaded through with blue, and they each wore a necklace of blue stones.

'To remind you of our first meeting!' teased Guy, kissing his bride on the way to Heathrow. They were spending two weeks in Switzerland, and would afterwards return to Cranleigh, which would be their home; Mrs Kent was delighted.

And so was Homer. He liked a man in the house.

Pack this alongside the suntan lotion

The lazy days of summer are evoked in 4 special new romances, set in warm, sunny countries.

Stories like Kerry Allyne's **"Carpentaria Moon"**, Penny Jordan's **"A new relationship"**, Roberta Leigh's **"A racy affair"**, and Jeneth Murrey's **"Bittersweet marriage"**.

Make sure the Holiday Romance Pack is top of your holiday list this summer.

AVAILABLE IN JUNE, PRICE £4.80

Doctor Nurse Romances

Romance in modern medical life

Read more about the lives and loves of doctors and nurses in the fascinatingly different backgrounds of contemporary medicine. These are the three Doctor Nurse romances to look out for next month.

CRUSADING CONSULTANT
Helen Upshall

DEAR DR SASSENACH
Kate Ashton

ANATOMY OF LOVE
Margaret Barker

Buy them from your usual paperback stockist, or write to: Mills & Boon Reader Service, P.O. Box 236, Thornton Rd, Croydon, Surrey CR9 3RU, England. Readers in Southern Africa — write to: Independent Book Services Pty, Postbag X3010, Randburg, 2125, S. Africa.

Mills & Boon
the rose of romance

A marriage for romance or revenge?

Twenty-one years ago Mario di Medici was murdered at sea. Many suspected it was James Tarleton's hand that had pushed him over the rail.

When his daughter, Chris Tarleton, came to Venice, the riddle of the past returned with her.

Before she knew how, she found herself married to Marcus di Medici, the dead man's son.

Was his marriage proposal intended to protect her from the shadowy figure that followed her every move?

Or was his motive revenge?

W☉RLDWIDE

Another title from the Worldwide range.

AVAILABLE FROM MAY 1987 PRICE £2.75
Available from Boots, Martins, John Menzies, W H Smiths, Woolworth's, and other paperback stockists.

Mills & Boon

YOU'RE INVITED TO ACCEPT
4 DOCTOR NURSE
ROMANCES
AND A TOTE BAG
FREE!

Doctor Nurse

Acceptance card

| NO STAMP NEEDED | Post to: **Reader Service, FREEPOST, P.O. Box 236, Croydon, Surrey. CR9 9EL** |

Please note readers in Southern Africa write to:
Independant Book Services P.T.Y., Postbag X3010, Randburg 2125, S. Africa

 YES! Please send me 4 free Doctor Nurse Romances and my free tote bag – and reserve a Reader Service Subscription for me. If I decide to subscribe I shall receive 6 new Doctor Nurse Romances every other month as soon as they come off the presses for £6.60 together with a FREE newsletter including information on top authors and special offers, exclusively for Reader Service subscribers. There are no postage and packing charges, and I understand I may cancel or suspend my subscription at any time. If I decide not to subscribe I shall write to you within 10 days. Even if I decide not to subscribe the 4 free novels and the tote bag are mine to keep forever. I am over 18 years of age   EP23D

NAME _____

(CAPITALS PLEASE)

ADDRESS _____

_____

—————————— **POSTCODE** ——————————

The right is reserved to refuse application and change the terms of this offer. You may be mailed with other offers as a result of this application. Offer expires September 30th 1987 and is limited to one per household.
Offer applies in UK and Eire only. Overseas send for details.